Mr. Meeson's Will

H. Rider Haggard

Alpha Editions

This edition published in 2023

ISBN : 9789357950497

Design and Setting By
Alpha Editions
www.alphaedis.com
Email - info@alphaedis.com

Contents

CHAPTER I.
AUGUSTA AND HER PUBLISHER.

Everybody who has any connection with Birmingham will be acquainted with the vast publishing establishment still known by the short title of "Meeson's," which is perhaps the most remarkable institution of the sort in Europe. There are—or rather there were, at the date of the beginning of this history—three partners in Meeson's—Meeson himself, the managing partner; Mr. Addison, and Mr. Roscoe—and people in Birmingham used to say that there were others interested in the affair, for Meeson's was a "company" (limited).

However this may be, Meeson and Co. was undoubtedly a commercial marvel. It employed more than two thousand hands; and its works, lit throughout with the electric light, cover two acres and a quarter of land. One hundred commercial travellers, at three pounds a week and a commission, went forth east and west, and north and south, to sell the books of Meeson (which were largely religious in their nature) in all lands; and five-and-twenty tame authors (who were illustrated by thirteen tame artists) sat—at salaries ranging from one to five hundred a year—in vault-like hutches in the basement, and week by week poured out that hat-work for which Meeson's was justly famous. Then there were editors and vice-editors, and heads of the various departments, and sub-heads, and financial secretaries, and readers, and many managers; but what their names were no man knew, because at Meeson's all the employees of the great house were known by numbers; personalities and personal responsibility being the abomination of the firm. Nor was it allowed to anyone having dealings with these items ever to see the same number twice, presumably for fear lest the number should remember that he was a man and a brother, and his heart should melt towards the unfortunate, and the financial interests of Meeson's should suffer. In short, Meeson's was an establishment created for and devoted to money-making, and the fact was kept studiously and even insolently before the eyes of everybody connected with it—which was, of course, as it should be, in this happy land of commerce. After all that has been written, the reader will not be surprised to learn that the partners in Meeson's were rich beyond the dreams of avarice. Their palaces would have been a wonder even in ancient Babylon, and would have excited admiration in the corruptest and most luxurious days of Rome. Where could one see such horses, such carriages, such galleries of sculpture or such collections of costly gems as at the palatial halls of Messrs. Meeson, Addison, and Roscoe?

"And to think," as the Mighty Meeson himself would say, with a lordly wave of his right hand, to some astonished wretch of an author whom he has chosen to overwhelm with the sight of this magnificence, "to think that all this comes out of the brains of chaps like you! Why, young man, I tell you that if all the money that has been paid to you scribblers since the days of Elizabeth were added together it would not come up to my little pile; but, mind you, it ain't so much fiction that has done the trick—it's religion. It's piety as pays, especially when it's printed."

Then the unsophisticated youth would go away, his heart too full for words, but pondering how these things were, and by-and-by he would pass into the Meeson melting-pot and learn something about it.

One day King Meeson sat in his counting house counting out his money, or, at least, looking over the books of the firm. He was in a very bad temper, and his heavy brows were wrinkled up in a way calculated to make the counting-house clerks shake on their stools. Meeson's had a branch establishment at Sydney, in Australia, which establishment had, until lately, been paying—it is true not as well as the English one, but, still, fifteen or twenty per cent. But now a wonder had come to pass. A great American publishing firm had started an opposition house in Melbourne, and their "cuteness" was more than the "cuteness" of Meeson. Did Meeson's publish an edition of the works of any standard author at threepence per volume the opposition company brought out the same work at twopence-halfpenny; did Meeson's subsidise a newspaper to puff their undertakings, the opposition firm subsidised two to cry them down, and so on. And now the results of all this were becoming apparent: for the financial year just ended the Australian branch had barely earned a beggarly net dividend of seven per cent.

No wonder Mr. Meeson was furious, and no wonder that the clerks shook upon their stools.

"This must be seen into, No. 3," said Mr. Meeson, bringing his fist down with a bang on to the balance-sheet.

No. 3 was one of the editors; a mild-eyed little man with blue spectacles. He had once been a writer of promise; but somehow Meeson's had got him for its own, and turned him into a publisher's hack.

"Quite so, Sir," he said humbly. "It is very bad—it is dreadful to think of Meeson's coming down to seven per cent—seven per cent!" and he held up his hands.

"Don't stand there like a stuck pig, No. 3," said Mr. Meeson, fiercely; "but suggest something."

"Well, Sir," said No. 3 more humbly than ever, for he was terribly afraid of his employer; "I think, perhaps, that somebody had better go to Australia, and see what can be done."

"I know one thing that can be done," said Mr. Meeson, with a snarl: "all those fools out there can be sacked, and sacked they shall be; and, what's more, I'll go and sack them myself. That will do No. 3; that will do;" and No. 3 departed, and glad enough he was to go.

As he went a clerk arrived, and gave a card to the great man.

"Miss Augusta Smithers," he read; then with a grunt, "show Miss Augusta Smithers in."

Presently Miss Augusta Smithers arrived. She was a tall, well-formed young lady of about twenty-five, with pretty golden hair, deep grey eyes, a fine forehead, and a delicate mouth; just now, however, she looked very nervous.

"Well, Miss Smithers, what is it?" asked the publisher.

"I came, Mr. Meeson—I came about my book."

"Your book, Miss Smithers?" this was an affectation of forgetfulness; "let me see?—forgive me, but we publish so many books. Oh, yes, I remember; 'Jemima's Vow.' Oh, well, I believe it is going on fairly."

"I saw you advertised the sixteenth thousand the other day," put in Miss Smithers, apologetically.

"Did we—did we? ah, then, you know more about it than I do," and he looked at his visitor in a way that conveyed clearly enough that he considered the interview was ended.

Miss Smithers rose, and then, with a spasmodic effort, sat down again. "The fact is, Mr. Meeson," she said—"The fact is, that, I thought that, perhaps, as 'Jemima's Vow' had been such a great success, you might, perhaps—in short, you might be inclined to give me some small sum in addition to what I have received."

Mr. Meeson looked up. His forehead was wrinkled till the shaggy eyebrows nearly hid the sharp little eyes.

"What!" he said. "*What!*"

At this moment the door opened, and a young gentleman came slowly in. He was a very nice-looking young man, tall and well shaped, with a fair skin and jolly blue eyes—in short, a typical young Englishman of the better sort, aetate suo twenty-four. I have said that he came slowly in, but that scarcely conveys the gay and *dégagé* air of independence which pervaded this young man, and which would certainly have struck any observer as little short of shocking, when contrasted with the worm-like attitude of those who crept round the feet of Meeson. This young man had not, indeed, even taken the trouble to remove his hat, which was stuck upon the back of his head, his hands were in his pockets, a sacrilegious whistle hovered on his lips, and he opened the door of the sanctum sanctorum of the Meeson establishment *with a kick*!

"How do, uncle?" he said to the Commercial Terror, who was sitting there behind his formidable books, addressing him even as though he were an ordinary man. "Why, what's up?"

Just then, however, he caught sight of the very handsome young lady who was seated in the office, and his whole demeanour underwent a most remarkable change; out came the hands from his pockets, off went the hat, and, turning, he bowed, really rather nicely, considering how impromptu the whole performance was.

"What is it, Eustace?" asked Mr. Meeson, sharply.

"Oh, nothing, uncle; nothing—it can bide," and, without waiting for an invitation, he took a chair, and sat down in such a position that he could see Miss Smithers without being seen of his uncle.

"I was saying, Miss Smithers, or rather, I was going to say," went on the elder Meeson, "that, in short, I do not in the least understand what you can mean. You will remember that you were paid a sum of fifty pounds for the copyright of 'Jemima's Vow.'"

"Great Heavens!" murmured Master Eustace, behind; "what a do!"

"At the time an alternative agreement, offering you seven per cent on the published price of the book, was submitted to you, and, had you accepted it, you would, doubtless, have realized a larger sum," and Mr. Meeson contracted his hairy eyebrows and gazed at the poor girl in a way that was, to say the least, alarming. But Augusta, though she felt sadly inclined to flee, still stood to her guns, for, to tell the truth, her need was very great.

"I could not afford to wait for the seven per cent, Mr. Meeson," she said humbly.

"Oh, ye gods! seven per cent, when he makes about forty-five!" murmured Eustace, in the background.

"Possibly, Miss Smithers; possibly;" went on the great man. "You must really forgive me if I am not acquainted with the exact condition of your private affairs. I am, however, aware from experience that the money matters of most writing people are a little embarrassed."

Augusta winced, and Mr. Meeson, rising heavily from his chair, went to a large safe which stood near, and extracted from it a bundle of agreements. These he glanced at one by one till he found what he was looking for.

"Here is the agreement," he said; "let me see? ah, I thought so—copyright fifty pounds, half proceeds of rights of translation, and a clause binding you to offer any future work you may produce during the next five years to our house on the seven per cent agreement, or a sum not exceeding one hundred pounds for the copyright. Now, Miss Smithers, what have you to say? You signed this paper of your own free will. It so happens that we have made a large profit on your book: indeed, I don't mind telling you that we have got as much as we gave you back from America for the sale of the American rights; but that is no ground for your coming to ask for more money than you agreed to accept. I never heard of such a thing in the whole course of my professional experience; never!" and he paused, and once more eyed her sternly.

"At any rate, there ought to be something to come to me from the rights of translation—I saw in the paper that the book was to be translated into French and German," said Augusta, faintly.

"Oh! yes, no doubt—Eustace, oblige me by touching the bell."

The young gentleman did so, and a tall, melancholy-looking clerk appeared.

"No. 18," snarled Mr. Meeson, in the tone of peculiar amiability that he reserved for his employés, "make out the translation account of 'Jemima's Vow,' and fill up a cheque of balance due to the author."

No. 18 vanished like a thin, unhappy ghost, and Mr. Meeson once more addressed the girl before him. "If you want money, Miss Smithers," he said, "you had better write us another book. I am not going to deny that your work is good work—a little too deep, and not quite orthodox enough, perhaps; but still good. I tested it myself, when it came to hand—which is a thing I don't often do—and saw it was good selling quality, and you see I didn't make a mistake. I believe 'Jemima's Vow' will sell twenty thousand without stopping—here's the account."

As he spoke the spectre-like clerk put down a neatly-ruled bit of paper and an unsigned cheque on the desk before his employer, and then smiled a shadowy smile and vanished.

Mr. Meeson glanced through the account, signed the cheque, and handed it, together with the account to Augusta, who proceeded to read it. It ran thus:—

AUGUSTA SMITHERS *in account with* MEESON & Co.

	£ s d
To Sale of Right of Translation of "Jemima's Vow" into French......	7 0 0

Do. do. do. into German	7 0 0
	————
	£14 0 0
	========
	£ s d
Less amount due to Messrs. Meeson, being one-half of net proceeds	7 0 0
Less Commission, &c	3 19 0
	————
	£10 19 0
	==========
Balance due to Author, as per cheque herewith.	£3 1 0
	————

Augusta looked, and then slowly crumpled up the cheque in her hand.

"If I understand, Mr. Meeson," she said, "you have sold the two rights of translation of my book, which you persuaded me to leave in your hands, for £14; out of which I am to receive £3 1s.?"

"Yes, Miss Smithers. Will you be so kind as to sign the receipt; the fact is that I have a good deal of business to attend to."

"No, Mr. Meeson," suddenly said Augusta, rising to her feet and looking exceedingly handsome and imposing in her anger. "No; I will not sign the receipt, and I will not take this cheque. And, what is more, I will not write you any more books. You have entrapped me. You have taken advantage of my ignorance and inexperience, and entrapped me so that for five years I shall be nothing but a slave to you, and, although I am now one of the most popular writers in the country, shall be obliged to accept a sum for my books upon which I cannot live. Do you know that yesterday I was offered a thousand pounds for the copyright of a book like 'Jemima's Vow'?—it's a large sum; but I have the letter. Yes, and I have the book in manuscript now; and if I could publish it I should be lifted out of poverty, together with my poor little sister!" and she gave a sob. "But," she went on, "I cannot publish it, and I will not let you have it and be treated like this; I had rather starve. I will publish nothing for five years, and I will write to the papers and say why—because I have been *cheated*, Mr. Meeson!"

"Cheated!" thundered the great man. "Be careful, young lady; mind what you are saying. I have a witness; Eustace, you hear, '*cheated*'! Eustace, '*cheated*'!"

"*I* hear," said Eustace, grimly.

"Yes, Mr. Meeson, I said '*cheated*'; and I will repeat it, whether I am locked up for it or not. Good morning, Mr. Meeson," and she curtseyed to him, and then suddenly burst into a flood of tears.

In a minute Eustace was by her side.

"Don't cry, Miss Smithers; for Heaven's sake, don't. I can't bear to see it," he said.

She looked up, her beautiful grey eyes full of tears, and tried to smile.

"Thank you," she said; "I am very silly, but I am so disappointed. If you only knew—. There, I will go. Thank you," and in another instant she had drawn herself up and left the room.

"Well," said Mr. Meeson, senior, who had been sitting at his desk with his great mouth open, apparently too much astonished to speak. "Well, there is a vixen for you. But she'll come round. I've known them to do that sort of thing before—there are one or two down there," and he jerked his thumb in the direction where the twenty and five tame authors sat each like a rabbit in his little hutch and did hat-work by the yard, "who carried on like that. But they are quiet enough now—they don't show much spirit now. I know how to deal with that sort of thing—half-pay and a double tale of copy—that's the ticket. Why, that girl will be worth fifteen hundred a year to the house. What do you think of it, young man, eh?"

"I think," answered his nephew, on whose good-tempered face a curious look of contempt and anger had gathered, "I think that you ought to be ashamed of yourself!"

CHAPTER II.
HOW EUSTACE WAS DISINHERITED.

There was a pause—a dreadful pause. The flash had left the cloud, but the answering thunder had not burst upon the ear. Mr. Meeson gasped. Then he took up the cheque which Augusta had thrown upon the table and slowly crumpled it.

"What did you say, young man?" he said at last, in a cold, hard voice.

"I said that you ought to be ashamed of yourself," answered his nephew, standing his ground bravely; "and, what is more, I meant it!"

"Oh! Now will you be so kind as to explain exactly why you said that, and why you meant it?"

"I meant it," answered his nephew, speaking in a full, strong voice, "because that girl was right when she said that you had cheated her, and you know that she was right. I have seen the accounts of 'Jemima's Vow'—I saw them this morning—and you have already made more than a thousand pounds clear profit on the book. And then, when she comes to ask you for something over the beggarly fifty pounds which you doled out to her, you refuse, and offer her three pounds as her share of the translation rights—three pounds as against your eleven!"

"Go on," interrupted his uncle; "pray go on."

"All right; I am going. That is not all: you actually avail yourself of a disgraceful trick to entrap this unfortunate girl into an agreement, whereby she becomes a literary bondslave for five years! As soon as you see that she has genius, you tell her that the expense of bringing out her book, and of advertising up her name, &c., &c., &c., will be very great—so great, indeed, that you cannot undertake it, unless, indeed, she agrees to let you have the first offer of everything she writes for five years to come, at somewhere about a fourth of the usual rate of a successful author's pay—though, of course, you don't tell her that. You take advantage of her inexperience to bind her by this iniquitous contract, knowing that the end of it will be that you will advance her a little money and get her into your power, and then will send her down there to the Hutches, where all the spirit and originality and genius will be crushed out of her work, and she will become a hat-writer like the rest of them—for Meeson's is a strictly commercial undertaking, you know, and Meeson's public don't like genius, they like their literature dull and holy!—and it's an infernal shame! that's what it is, uncle!" and the young man, whose blue eyes were by this time flashing fire, for he had worked himself up as he went along, brought his fist down with a bang upon the writing table by way of emphasising his words.

"Have you done?" said his uncle.

"Yes, I've done; and I hope that I have put it plain."

"Very well; and now might I ask you, supposing that you should ever come to manage this business, if your sentiments accurately represent the system upon which you would proceed?"

"Of course they do. I am not going to turn cheat for anybody."

"Thank you. They seem to have taught you the art of plain speaking up at Oxford—though, it appears," with a sneer, "they taught you very little else. Well, then, now it is my turn to speak; and I tell you what it is, young man, you will either instantly beg my pardon for what you have said, or you will leave Meeson's for good and all."

"I won't beg your pardon for speaking the truth," said Eustace, hotly: "the fact is that here you never hear the truth; all these poor devils creep and crawl about you, and daren't call their souls their own. I shall be devilish glad to get out of this place, I can tell you. All this chickery and pokery makes me sick. The place stinks and reeks of sharp practice and money-making—money-making by fair means or foul."

The elder man had, up till now, at all events to outward appearance, kept his temper; but this last flower of vigorous English was altogether too much for one whom the possession of so much money had for many years shielded from hearing unpleasant truths put roughly. The man's face grew like a devil's, his thick eyebrows contracted themselves, and his pale lips quivered with fury. For a few seconds he could not speak, so great was his emotion. When, at length, he did, his voice was as thick and laden with rage as a dense mist is with rain.

"You impudent young rascal!" he began, "you ungrateful foundling! Do you suppose that when my brother left you to starve—which was all that you were fit for—I picked you out of the gutter for this: that you should have the insolence to come and tell me how to conduct my business? Now, young man, I'll just tell you what it is. You can be off and conduct a business of your own on whatever principles you choose. Get out of Meeson's, Sir; and never dare to show your nose here again, or I'll give the porters orders to hustle you off the premises! And, now, that isn't all. I've done with you, never you look to me for another sixpence! I'm not going to support you any longer, I can tell you. And, what's more, do you know what I'm going to do just now? I'm going off to old Todd—that's my lawyer—and I'm going to tell him to make another will and to leave every farthing I have—and that isn't much short of two millions, one way and another—to Addison and Roscoe. They don't want it, but that don't matter. You shan't have it—no, not a farthing of it; and I won't have a pile like that frittered away in charities and mismanagement. There now, my fine young gentleman, just be off and see if your new business principles will get you a living."

"All right, uncle; I'm going," said the young man, quietly. "I quite understand what our quarrel means for me, and, to tell you the truth, I am not sorry. I have never wished to be dependent on you, or to have anything to do with a business carried on as Meeson's is. I have a hundred a year my mother left me, and with the help of that and my education, I hope to make a living. Still, I don't want to part from you in anger, because you have been very kind to me at times, and, as you remind me, you picked me out of the gutter when I was orphaned or not far from it. So I hope you will shake hands before I go."

"Ah!" snarled his uncle; "you want to pipe down now, do you? But that won't do. Off you go! and mind you don't set foot in Pompadour Hall," Mr. Meeson's seat, "unless it is to get your clothes. Come, cut!"

"You misunderstand me," said Eustace, with a touch of native dignity which became him very well. "Probably we shall not meet again, and I did not wish to part in anger, that was all. Good morning." And he bowed and left the office.

"Confound him!" muttered his uncle as the door closed, "he's a good plucked one—showed spirit. But I'll show spirit, too. Meeson is a man of his word. Cut him off with a shilling? not I; cut him off with nothing at all. And yet, curse it, I like the lad. Well, I've done with him, thanks to that minx of a Smithers girl. Perhaps he's sweet on her? then they can go and starve together, and be hanged to them! She had better keep out of my way, for she shall smart for this, so sure as my name is Jonathan Meeson. I'll keep her up to the letter of that agreement, and, if she tries to publish a book inside of this country or out of it, I'll crush her—yes, I'll crush her, if it cost me five thousand to do it!" and, with a snarl, he dropped his fist heavily upon the table before him.

Then he rose, put poor Augusta's agreement carefully back into the safe, which he shut with a savage snap, and proceeded to visit the various departments of his vast establishment, and to make such hay therein as had never before been dreamt of in the classic halls of Meeson's.

To this hour the clerks of the great house talk of that dreadful day with bated breath—for as bloody Hector raged through the Greeks, so did the great Meeson rage through his hundred departments. In the very first office he caught a wretched clerk eating sardine sandwiches. Without a moment's hesitation he took the sandwiches and threw them through the window.

"Do you suppose I pay you to come and eat your filthy sandwiches here?" he asked savagely. "There, now you can go and look for them; and see you here: you needn't trouble to come back, you idle, worthless fellow. Off you go! and remember you need not send to me for a character. Now then—double quick!"

The unfortunate departed, feebly remonstrating, and Meeson, having glared around at the other clerks and warned them that unless they were careful—very careful—they would soon follow in his tracks, continued his course of devastation.

Presently he met an editor, No. 7 it was, who was bringing him an agreement to sign. He snatched it from him and glanced through it.

"What do you mean by bringing me a thing like this?" he said: "It's all wrong."

"It is exactly as you dictated to me yesterday, Sir," said the editor indignantly.

"What, do you mean to contradict me?" roared Meeson. "Look here No. 7, you and I had better part. Now, no words: your salary will be paid to you till the end of the month, and if you would like to bring an action for wrongful dismissal, why, I'm your man. Good morning, No. 7; good morning."

Next he crossed a courtyard where, by slipping stealthily around the corner, he came upon a jolly little errand boy, who was enjoying a solitary game of marbles.

Whack came his cane across the seat of that errand boy's trousers, and in another minute he had followed the editor and the sandwich-devouring clerk.

And so the merry game went on for half an hour or more, till at last Mr. Meeson was fain to cease his troubling, being too exhausted to continue his destroying course. But next morning there was promotion going on in the great publishing house; eleven vacancies had to be filled.

A couple of glasses of brown sherry and a few sandwiches, which he hastily swallowed at a neighboring restaurant, quickly restored him, however; and, jumping into a cab, he drove post haste to his lawyers', Messrs. Todd and James.

"Is Mr. Todd in?" he said to the managing clerk, who came forward bowing obsequiously to the richest man in Birmingham.

"Mr. Todd will be disengaged in a few minutes, Sir," he said. "May I offer you the *Times*?"

"Damn the *Times*!" was the polite answer; "I don't come here to read newspapers. Tell Mr. Todd I must see him at once, or else I shall go elsewhere."

"I am much afraid Sir"—began the managing clerk.

Mr. Meeson jumped up and grabbed his hat. "Now then, which is it to be?" he said.

"Oh, certainly, Sir; pray be seated," answered the manager in great alarm—Meeson's business was not a thing to be lightly lost. "I will see Mr. Todd instantly," and he vanished.

Almost simultaneously with his departure an old lady was unceremoniously bundled out of an inner room, clutching feebly at a reticule full of papers and proclaiming loudly that her head was going round and round. The poor old soul was just altering her will for the eighteenth time in favor of a brand new charity, highly recommended by Royalty; and to be suddenly shot from the revered presence of her lawyer out into the outer darkness of the clerk's office, was really too much for her.

In another minute, Mr. Meeson was being warmly, even enthusiastically, greeted by Mr. Todd himself. Mr. Todd was a nervous-looking, jumpy little man, who spoke in jerks and gushes in such a way as to remind one of a fire-hose through which water was being pumped intermittently.

"How do you do, my dear Sir? Delighted to have this pleasure," he began with a sudden gush, and then suddenly dried up, as he noticed the ominous expression on the great man's brow. "I am sure I am very sorry that you were kept waiting, my dear Sir: but I was at the moment engaged with an excellent and most Christian testator."—

Here he suddenly jumped and dried up again, for Mr. Meeson, without the slightest warning, ejaculated: "Curse your Christian testator! And look here, Todd, just you see that it does not happen again. I'm a Christian testator too; and Christians of my cut aren't accustomed to be kept standing about just like office-boys or authors. See that it don't happen again, Todd."

"I am sure I am exceedingly grieved. Circumstances"—

"Oh, never mind all that—I want my will."

"Will—will—Forgive me—a little confused, that's all. Your manner is so full of hearty old middle-age's kind of vigour"—

Here he stopped, more suddenly even than usual, for Mr. Meeson fixed him with his savage eye, and then jerked himself out of the room to look for the document in question.

"Little idiot!" muttered Meeson; "I'll give him the sack, too, if he isn't more careful. By Jove! why should I not have my own resident solicitor? I could get a sharp hand with a damaged character for about £300 a year, and I pay that old Todd quite £2000. There is a vacant place in the Hutches that I could turn into an office. Hang me, if I don't do it. I will make that little chirping grasshopper jump to some purpose, I'll warrant," and he chuckled at the idea.

Just then Mr. Todd returned with the will, and before he could begin to make any explanations his employer cut him short with a sharp order to read the gist of it.

This the lawyer proceeded to do. It was very short, and, with the exception of a few legacies, amounting in all to about twenty thousand pounds, bequeathed all the testator's vast fortune and estates, including his (by far the largest) interest in the great publishing house, and his palace with the paintings and other valuable contents, known as Pompadour Hall, to his nephew, Eustace H. Meeson.

"Very well," he said, when the reading was finished; "now give it to me."

Mr. Todd obeyed, and handed the document to his patron, who deliberately rent it into fragments with his strong fingers, and then completed its destruction by tearing it with his big white teeth. This done, he mixed the little pieces up, threw them on the floor, and stamped upon them with an air of malignity that almost frightened jerky little Mr. Todd.

"Now then," he grimly said, "there's an end of the old love; so let's on with the new. Take your pen and receive my instructions for my will."

Mr. Todd did as he was bid.

"I leave all my property, real and personal, to be divided in equal shares between my two partners, Alfred Tom Addison and Cecil Spooner Roscoe. There, that's short and sweet, and, one way and another, means a couple of millions."

"Good heavens! Sir," jerked out Mr. Todd. "Why, do you mean to quite cut out your nephew—and the other legatees?" he added by way of an afterthought.

"Of course I do; that is, as regards my nephew. The legatees may stand as before."

"Well all I have to say," went on the little man, astonished into honesty, "Is that it is the most shameful thing I ever heard of!"

"Indeed, Mr. Todd, is it? Well now, may I ask you: am I leaving this property, or are you? Don't trouble yourself to answer that, however, but just attend. Either you draw up that will at once, while I wait, or you say good-bye to about £2000 a year, for that's what Meeson's business is worth, I reckon. Now you take your choice."

Mr. Todd did take his choice. In under an hour, the will, which was very short, was drawn and engrossed.

"Now then," said Meeson, addressing himself to Mr. Todd and the managing clerk, as he took the quill between his fingers to sign, "do you two bear in mind that at the moment I execute this will I am of sound mind, memory, and understanding. There you are; now do you two witness."

It was night, and King capital, in the shape of Mr. Meeson, sat alone at dinner in his palatial dining-room at Pompadour. Dinner was over, the powdered footman had departed with stately tread, and the head butler was just placing the decanters of richly coloured wine before the solitary lord of all. The dinner had been a melancholy failure. Dish after dish, the cost of any one of which would have fed a poor child for a month, had been brought up and handed to the master only to be found fault with and sent away. On that night Mr. Meeson had no appetite.

"Johnson," he said to the butler, when he was sure the footman could not hear him, "has Mr. Eustace been here?"

"Yes, Sir."

"Has he gone?"

"Yes, Sir. He came to fetch his things, and then went away in a cab."

"Where to?"

"I don't know, Sir. He told the man to drive to Birmingham."

"Did he leave any message?"

"Yes, Sir, he bade me say that you should not be troubled with him again; but that he was sorry that you had parted from him in anger."

"Why did you not give me that message before?"

"Because Mr. Eustace said I was not to give it unless you asked after him."

"Very good. Johnson!"

"Yes, Sir."

"You will give orders that Mr. Eustace's name is not to be mentioned in this house again. Any servant mentioning Mr. Eustace's name will be dismissed."

"Very good, Sir"; and Johnson went.

Mr. Meeson gazed round him. He looked at the long array of glass and silver, at the spotless napery and costly flowers. He looked at the walls hung with works of art, which, whatever else they might be, were at least expensive; at the mirrors and the soft wax-lights; at the marble mantelpieces and the bright warm fires (for it was November); at the rich wall paper and the soft, deep-hued carpet; and reflected that they were all his. And then he sighed, and his coarse, heavy face sank in and grew sad. Of what use was this last extremity of luxury to him? He had nobody to leave it to, and to speak the truth, it gave him but little pleasure. Such pleasure as he had in life was derived from making money, not from spending it. The only times when he was really happy were when he was in his counting house directing the enterprises of his vast establishment, and adding sovereign by sovereign to his enormous accumulations. That had been his one joy for forty years, and it was still his joy.

And then he fell to thinking of his nephew, the only son of his brother, whom he had once loved, before he lost himself in publishing books and making money, and sighed. He had been attached to the lad in his own coarse way, and it was a blow to him to cut himself loose from him. But Eustace had defied him, and—what was worse—he had told him the truth, which he, of all men, could not bear. He had said that his system of trade was dishonest, that he took more than his due, and it was so. He knew it; but he could not tolerate that it should be told him, and that his whole life should thereby be discredited, and even his accumulated gold tarnished—stamped as ill-gotten; least of all could he bear it from his dependent. He was not altogether a bad man; nobody is; he was only a coarse, vulgar tradesman, hardened and defiled by a long career of sharp dealing. At the bottom, he had his feelings like other men, but he could not tolerate exposure or even contradiction; therefore he had revenged himself. And yet, as he sat there, in solitary glory, he realized that to revenge does not bring happiness, and could even find it in his heart to envy the steadfast honesty that had defied him at the cost of his own ruin.

Not that he meant to relent or alter his determination. Mr. Meeson never relented, and never changed his mind. Had he done so he would not at that moment have been the master of two millions of money.

CHAPTER III.
AUGUSTA'S LITTLE SISTER.

When Augusta left Meeson's she was in a very sad condition of mind, to explain which it will be necessary to say a word or two about that young lady's previous history. Her father had been a clergyman, and, like most clergymen, not overburdened with the good things of this world. When Mr. Smithers—or, rather, the Rev. James Smithers—had died, he left behind him a widow and two children—Augusta, aged fourteen, and Jeannie, aged two. There had been two others, both boys, who had come into the world between Augusta and Jeannie, but they had both preceded their father to the land of shadows. Mrs. Smithers, had, fortunately for herself, a life interest in a sum of £7000, which, being well invested, brought her in £350 a year: and, in order to turn this little income to the best possible account and give her two girls the best educational opportunities possible under the circumstances, she, on her husband's death, moved from the village where he had for many years been curate, into the city of Birmingham. Here she lived in absolute retirement for some seven years and then suddenly died, leaving the two girls, then respectively nineteen and eight years of age, to mourn her loss, and, friendless as they were, to fight their way in the hard world.

Mrs. Smithers had been a saving woman, and, on her death, it was found that, after paying all debts, there remained a sum of £600 for the two girls to live on, and nothing else; for their mother's fortune died with her. Now, it will be obvious that the interest arising from six hundred pounds is not sufficient to support two young people, and therefore Augusta was forced to live upon the principal. From an early age, however, she (Augusta) had shown a strong literary tendency, and shortly after her mother's death she published her first book at her own expense. It was a dead failure and cost her fifty-two pounds, the balance between the profit and loss account. After awhile, however, she recovered from this blow, and wrote "Jemima's Vow," which was taken up by Meeson's; and, strange as it may seem, proved the success of the year. Of the nature of the agreement into which she entered with Meeson's, the reader is already acquainted, and he will not therefore be surprised to learn that under its cruel provisions Augusta, notwithstanding her name and fame, was absolutely prohibited from reaping the fruits of her success. She could only publish with Meesons's, and at the fixed pay of seven per cent on the advertised price of her work. Now, something over three years had elapsed since the death of Mrs. Smithers, and it will therefore be obvious that there was not much remaining of the six hundred pounds which she had left behind her. The two girls had, indeed, lived economically enough in a couple of small rooms in a back street; but their expenses had been enormously increased by the serious illness, from a pulmonary complaint, of the little girl Jeannie, now a child between twelve and thirteen years of age. On that morning, Augusta had seen the doctor and been crushed into the dust by the expression of his conviction, that, unless her little sister was moved to a warmer climate, for a period of at least a year, she would not live through the winter, and *might* die at any moment.

Take Jeannie to a warmer climate! He might as well have told Augusta to take her to the moon. Alas, she had not the money and did not know where to turn to get it! Oh! reader, pray to Heaven that it may never be your lot to see your best beloved die for the want of a few hundred pounds wherewith to save her life!

It was in this terrible emergency that she had—driven thereto by her agony of mind—tried to get something beyond her strict and legal due out of Meeson's—Meeson's that had made hundreds and hundreds out of her book and paid her fifty pounds. We know how she fared in that attempt. On leaving their office, Augusta bethought her of her banker. Perhaps he might be willing to advance something. It was a horrible task, but she determined to undertake it; so she walked to the bank and asked to see the manager. He was out, but would be in at three o'clock. She went to a shop near and got a bun and glass of milk, and waited till she was ashamed to wait any longer, and then she walked about the streets till three o'clock. At the stroke of the hour she returned, and was shown into the manager's private room, where a dry, unsympathetic looking little man was sitting before a big book. It was not the same man whom Augusta had met before, and her heart sank proportionately.

What followed need not be repeated here. The manager listened to her faltering tale with a few stereotyped expressions of sympathy, and, when she had done, "regretted" that speculative loans were contrary to the custom of the bank, and politely bowed her out.

It was nearly four o'clock upon a damp, drizzling afternoon—a November afternoon—that hung like a living misery over the black slush of the Birmingham streets, and would in itself have sufficed to bring the lightest hearted, happiest mortal to the very gates of despair, when Augusta, wet, wearied, and almost crying, at last entered the door of their little sitting-room. She entered very quietly, for the maid-of-all-work had met her in the passage and told her that Miss Jeannie was asleep. She had been coughing very much about dinner-time, but now she was asleep.

There was a fire in the grate, a small one, for the coal was economised by means of two large fire-bricks, and on a table (Augusta's writing table), placed at the further side of the room, was a paraffin-lamp turned low. Drawn up in front, but a little to one side of the fire, was a sofa, covered with red rep, and on the sofa lay a fair-haired little form, so thin and fragile that it looked like the ghost or outline of a girl, rather than a girl herself. It was Jeannie, her sick sister, and she was asleep. Augusta stole softly up to look at her. It was a sweet little face that her eyes fell on, although it was so shockingly thin, with long, curved lashes, delicate nostrils, and a mouth shaped like a bow. All the lines and grooves which the chisel of Pain knows so well how to carve were smoothed out of it now, and in their place lay the shadow of a smile.

Augusta looked at her and clenched her fists, while a lump rose in her throat, and her grey eyes filled with tears. How could she get the money to save her? The year before a rich man, a man who was detestable to her, had wanted to marry her, and she would have nothing to say to him. He had gone abroad, else she would have gone back to him and married him—at a price. Marry him? yes she would marry him: she would do anything for money to take her sister away! What did she care for herself when her darling was dying—dying for the want of two hundred pounds!

Just then Jeannie woke up, and stretched her arms out to her.

"So you are back at last, dear," she said in her sweet childish voice. "It has been so lonely without you. Why, how wet you are! Take off your jacket at once, Gussie, or you will soon be as ill as"—and here she broke out into a terrible fit of coughing, that seemed to shake her tender frame as the wind shakes a reed.

Her sister turned and obeyed, and then came and sat by the sofa and took the thin little hand in hers.

"Well, Gussie, and how did you get on with the Printer-devil" (this was her impolite name for the great Meeson); "will he give you any more money?"

"No, dear; we quarrelled, that was all, and I came away."

"Then I suppose that we can't go abroad?"

Augusta was too moved to answer; she only shook her head. The child buried her face in the pillow and gave a sob or two. Presently she was quiet, and lifted it again. "Gussie, love," she said, "don't be angry, but I want to speak to you. Listen, my sweet Gussie, my angel. Oh, Gussie, you don't know how I love you! It is all no good, it is useless struggling against it, I must die sooner or later; though I am only twelve, and you think me such a child, I am old enough to understand that. I think," she added, after pausing to cough, "that pain makes one old: I feel as though I were fifty. Well, so you see I may as well give up fighting against it and die at once. I am only a burden and anxiety to you—I may as well die at once and go to sleep."

"Don't, Jeannie! don't!" said her sister, in a sort of cry; "you are killing me!"

Jeannie laid her hot hand upon Augusta's arm, "Try and listen to me, dear," she said, "even if it hurts, because I do so want to say something. Why should you be so frightened about me? Can any place that I can go be worse than this place? Can I suffer more pain anywhere, or be more hurt when I see you crying? Think how wretched it has all been. There has only been one beautiful thing in our lives for years and years, and that was your book. Even when I am feeling worst—when my chest aches, you know—I grow quite happy when I think of what the papers wrote about you: the *Times* and the *Saturday Review*, and the *Spectator*, and the rest of them. They said that you had genius—true genius, you remember, and that they expected one day to see you at the head of the literature of the time, or near it. The Printer-devil can't take away that, Gussie. He can take the money; but he can't say that he wrote the book; though," she added, with a touch of childish spite and vivacity, "I have no doubt that he would if he could. And then there were those letters from the great authors up in London; yes, I often think of them too. Well, dearest old girl, the best of it is that I know it is all true. I *know*, I can't tell you how, that you will be a great woman in spite of all the Meesons in creation; for somehow you will get out of his power, and, if you don't, five years is not all one's life—at least, not if people have a life. At the worst, he can only take all the money. And then, when you are great and rich and famous, and more beautiful than ever, and when the people turn their heads as you come into the room, like we used to at school when the missionary came to lecture, I know that you will think of me (because you won't forget me as some sisters do), and of how, years and years before, so long ago that the time looks quite small when you think of it, I told you that it would be so just before I died."

Here the girl, who had been speaking with a curious air of certainty and with a gravity and deliberation extraordinary for one so young, suddenly broke off to cough. Her sister threw herself on her knees beside her, and, clasping her in her arms, implored her in broken accents not to talk of dying. Jeannie drew Augusta's golden head down on her breast and stroked it.

"Very well, Gussie, I won't say any more about it," she said; "but it is no good hiding the truth, dear. I am tired of fighting against it; it is no good—none at all. Anyhow we have loved each other very much, dear; and perhaps—somewhere else—we may again."—And the brave little heart again broke down, and, overcome by the prescience of approaching separation, they both sobbed bitterly there upon the sofa. Presently came a knock at the door, and Augusta sprang up and turned to hide her tears. It was the maid-of-all-work bringing the tea; and, as she came blundering in, a sense of the irony of things forced itself into Augusta's soul. Here they were plunged into the most terrible sorrow, weeping at the inevitable approach of that chill end, and still appearances must be kept up, even before a maid-of-all-work. Society, even when represented by a maid-of-all-work, cannot do away with the intrusion of domestic griefs, or any other griefs, and in our hearts we know it and act up to it. Far gone, indeed, must we be in mental or physical agony before we abandon the attempt to keep up appearances.

Augusta drank a little tea and ate a very small bit of bread-and-butter. As in the case of Mr. Meeson, the events of the day had not tended to increase her appetite. Jeannie drank a little milk but ate nothing. When this form had been gone through, and the maid-of-all-work had once more made her appearance and cleared the table, Jeannie spoke again.

"Gus," she said, "I want you to put me to bed and then come and read to me out of 'Jemima's Vow'—where poor Jemima dies, you know. It is the most beautiful thing in the book, and I want to hear it again."

Her sister did as she wished, and, taking down "Jemima's Vow," Jeannie's *own* copy as it was called, being the very first that had come into the house, she opened it at the part Jeannie had asked for and read aloud, keeping her voice as steady as she could. As a matter of fact, however, the scene itself was as powerful as it was pathetic, and quite sufficient to account for any unseemly exhibitions of feeling on the part of the reader. However, she struggled through it till the last sentence was reached. It ran thus:—"And so Jemima stretched out her hand to him and said 'Good-bye.' And presently, knowing that she had now kept her promise, and being happy because she had done so, she went to sleep."

"Ah!" murmured the blue-eyed child who listened. "I wish that I was as good as Jemima. But though I have no vow to keep I can say 'Good-bye,' and I can go to sleep."

Augusta made no answer, and presently Jeannie dozed off. Her sister looked at her with eager affection. "She is giving up," she said to herself, "and, if she gives up, she will die. I know it, it is because we are not going away. How can I get the money, now that that horrible man is gone? how can I get it?" and she buried her head in her hand and thought. Presently an idea struck her: she might go back to Meeson and eat her words, and sell him the copyright of her new book for £100, as the agreement provided. That would not be enough, however; for travelling with an invalid is expensive; but she might offer to bind herself over to him for a term of years as a tame author, like those who worked in the Hutches. She was sure that he would be glad to get her, if only he could do so at his own price. It would be slavery worse than any penal servitude, and even now she shudders at the prospect of prostituting her great abilities to the necessities of such work as Meeson's made their thousands out of—work out of which every spark of originality was stamped into nothingness, as though it were the mark of the Beast. Yes, it would be dreadful—it would break her heart; but she was prepared to have her heart broken and her genius wrung out of her by inches, if only she could get two hundred pounds wherewith to take Jeannie away to the South of France. Mr. Meeson would, no doubt, make a hard bargain—the hardest he could; but still, if she would consent to bind herself for a sufficient number of years at a sufficiently low salary, he would probably advance her a hundred pounds, besides the hundred for the copyright of the new book.

And so having made up her mind to the sacrifice, she went to bed, and, wearied out with misery, to sleep. And even as she slept, a Presence that she could not see was standing near her bed, and a Voice that she could not hear was calling through the gloom. Another mortal had bent low at the feet of that Unknown God whom men name Death, and been borne away on his rushing pinions into the spaces of the Hid. One more human item lay still and stiff, one more account was closed for good or evil, the echo of one more tread had passed from the earth for ever. The old million-numbered tragedy in which all must take a part had repeated itself once more down to its last and most awful scene. Yes; the grim farce was played out, and the little actor Jeannie was white in death!

Just at the dawn, Augusta dreamed that somebody with cold breath was breathing on her face, and woke up with a start and listened. Jeannie's bed was on the other side of the room, and she could generally hear her movements plainly enough, for the sick child was a restless sleeper. But now she could hear nothing, not even the faint vibration of her sister's breath. The silence was absolute and appalling; it struck tangibly upon her sense, as the darkness struck upon her eye-balls and filled her with a numb, unreasoning terror. She slipped out of bed and struck a match. In another few seconds she was standing by Jeannie's white little bed, waiting for the wick of the candle to burn up. Presently the light grew. Jeannie was lying on her side, her white face resting on her white arm. Her eyes were wide open; but when Augusta held the candle near her she did not shut them or flinch. Her hand, too—oh, Heavens! the fingers were nearly cold.

Then Augusta understood, and lifting up her arms in agony, she shrieked till the whole house rang.

CHAPTER IV.
AUGUSTA'S DECISION.

On the second day following the death of poor little Jeannie Smithers, Mr. Eustace Meeson was strolling about Birmingham with his hands in his pockets, and an air of indecision on his decidedly agreeable and gentlemanlike countenance. Eustace Meeson was not particularly cast down by the extraordinary reverse of fortune which he had recently experienced. He was a young gentleman of a cheerful nature; and, besides, it did not so very much matter to him. He was in a blessed condition of celibacy, and had no wife and children dependent upon him, and he knew that, somehow or other, it would go hard if, with the help of the one hundred a year that he had of his own, he did not manage, with his education, to get a living by hook or by crook. So it was not the loss of the society of his respected uncle, or the prospective enjoyment of two millions of money, which was troubling him. Indeed, after he had once cleared his goods and chattels out of Pompadour Hall and settled them in a room in an Hotel, he had not given the matter much thought. But he had given a good many thoughts to Augusta Smithers' grey eyes and, by way of getting an insight into her character, he had at once invested in a copy of "Jemima's Vow," thereby, somewhat against his will, swelling the gains of Meeson's to the extent of several shillings. Now, "Jemima's Vow," though simple and homely, was a most striking and powerful book, which fully deserved the reputation that it had gained, and it affected Eustace—who was in so much different from most young men of his age that he really did know the difference between good work and bad—more strongly than he would have liked to own. Indeed, at the termination of the story, what between the beauty of Augusta's pages, the memory of Augusta's eyes, and the knowledge of Augusta's wrongs, Mr. Eustace Meeson began to feel very much as though he had fallen in love. Accordingly, he went out walking, and meeting a clerk whom he had known in the Meeson establishment—one of those who had been discharged on the same day as himself—he obtained from him Miss Smithers' address, and began to reflect as to whether or no he should call upon her. Unable to make up his mind, he continued to walk till he reached the quiet street where Augusta lived, and, suddenly perceiving the house of which the clerk had told him, yielded to temptation and rang.

The door was answered by the maid-of-all-work, who looked at him a little curiously, but said that Miss Smithers was in, and then conducted him to a door which was half open, and left him in that kindly and agreeable fashion that maids-of-all-work have. Eustace was perplexed, and, looking through the door to see if anyone was in the room, discovered Augusta herself dressed in some dark material, seated in a chair, her hands folded on her lap, her pale face set like a stone, and her eyes gleaming into vacancy. He paused, wondering what could be the matter, and as he did so his umbrella slipped from his hand, making a noise that rendered it necessary for him to declare himself.

Augusta rose as he advanced, and looked at him with a puzzled air, as though she was striving to recall his name or where she had met him.

"I beg your pardon," he stammered, "I must introduce myself, as the girl has deserted me—I am Eustace Meeson."

Augusta's face hardened at the name. "If you have come to me from Messrs. Meeson and Co."—she said quickly, and then broke off, as though struck by some new idea.

"Indeed, no," said Eustace. "I have nothing in common with Messrs. Meeson now, except my name, and I have only come to tell you how sorry I was to see you treated as you were by my uncle. You remember I was in the office?"

"Yes," she said, with a suspicion of a blush, "I remember you were very kind."

"Well, you see," he went on, "I had a great row with my uncle after that, and it ended in his turning me out of the place, bag and baggage, and informing me that he was going to cut me off with a shilling, which," he added reflectively, "he has probably done by now."

"Do I understand you, Mr. Meeson, to mean that you quarrelled with your uncle about me and my books?"

"Yes; that is so," he said.

"It was very chivalrous of you," she answered, looking at him with a new-born curiosity. Augusta was not accustomed to find knights-errant thus prepared, at such cost to themselves, to break a lance in her cause. Least of all was she prepared to find that knight bearing the hateful crest of Meeson—if, indeed, Meeson had a crest.

"I ought to apologise," she went on presently, after an awkward pause, "for making such a scene in the office, but I wanted money so dreadfully, and it was so hard to be refused. But it does not matter now. It is all done with."

There was a dull, hopeless ring about her voice that awoke his curiosity. For what could she have wanted the money, and why did she no longer want it?

"I am sorry," he said. "Will you tell me what you wanted it so much for?"

She looked at him, and then, acting upon impulse rather then reflection, said in a low voice,

"If you like, I will show you."

He bowed, wondering what was coming next. Rising from her chair, Augusta led the way to a door which opened out of the sitting-room, and gently turned the handle and entered. Eustace followed her. The room was a small bed-room, of which the faded calico blind had been pulled down; as it happened, however, the sunlight, such as it was, beat full upon the blind, and came through it in yellow bars. They fell upon the furniture of the bare little room, they fell upon the iron bedstead, and upon something lying on it, which he did not at first notice, because it was covered with a sheet.

Augusta walked up to the bed and gently lifted the sheet, revealing the sweet face, fringed round about with golden hair, of little Jeannie, in her coffin.

Eustace gave an exclamation, and started back violently. He had not been prepared for such a sight; indeed it was the first such sight that he had ever seen, and it shocked him beyond words. Augusta, familiarised as she was herself with the companionship of this beauteous clay cold Terror, had forgotten that, suddenly and without warning to bring the living into the presence of the dead, is not the wisest or the kindest thing to do. For, to the living, more especially to the young, the sight of death is horrible. It is such a fearsome comment on their health and strength. Youth and strength are merry; but who can be merry with yon dead thing in the upper chamber? Take it away! thrust it underground! it is an insult to us; it reminds us that we, too, die like others. What business has its pallor to show itself against our ruddy cheeks?

"I beg your pardon," whispered Augusta, realising something of all this in a flash, "I forgot, you do not know—you must be shocked—Forgive me!"

"Who is it?" he said, gasping to get back his breath.

"My sister," she answered. "It was to try and save her life that I wanted the money. When I told her that I could not get it, she gave up and died. Your uncle killed her. Come."

Greatly shocked, he followed her back into the sitting-room, and then—as soon as he got his composure—apologised for having intruded himself upon her in such an hour of desolation.

"I am glad to see you," she said simply, "I have seen nobody except the doctor once, and the undertaker twice. It is dreadful to sit alone hour after hour face to face with the irretrievable. If I had not been so foolish as to enter into that agreement with Messrs. Meeson, I could have got the money by selling my new book easily enough; and I should have been able to take Jeannie abroad, and I believe that she would have lived—at least I hoped so. But now it is finished, and cannot be helped."

"I wish I had known," blundered Eustace, "I could have lent you the money. I have a hundred and fifty pounds."

"You are very good," she answered gently, "but it is no use talking about it now, it is finished."

Then Eustace rose and went away; and it was not till he found himself in the street that he remembered that he had never asked Augusta what her plans were. Indeed, the sight of poor Jeannie had put everything else out of his head. However, he consoled himself with the reflection that he could call again a week or ten days after the funeral.

Two days later, Augusta followed the remains of her dearly beloved sister to their last resting place, and then came home on foot (for she was the only mourner), and sat in her black gown before the little fire, and reflected upon her position. What was she to do? She could not stay in these rooms. It made her heart ache every time her eyes fell upon the empty sofa opposite, dinted as it was with the accustomed weight of poor Jeannie's frame. Where was she to go, and what was she to do. She might get literary employment, but then her agreement with Messrs. Meeson stared her in the face. That agreement was very widely drawn. It bound her to offer all literary work of any sort, that might come from her pen during the next five years, to Messrs. Meeson at the fixed rate of seven per cent, on the published price. Obviously, as it seemed to her, though perhaps erroneously, this clause might be stretched to include even a newspaper article, and she knew the malignant nature of Mr. Meeson well enough to be quite certain that, if possible, that would be done. It was true she might manage to make a bare living out of her work, even at the beggarly pay of seven per cent, but Augusta was a person of spirit, and determined that she would rather starve than that Meeson should again make huge profits out of her labour. This avenue being closed to her, she turned her mind elsewhere; but, look where she might, the prospect was equally dark.

Augusta's remarkable literary success had not been of much practical advantage to her, for in this country literary success does not mean so much as it does in some others. As a matter of fact, indeed, the average Briton has, at heart, a considerable contempt, if not for literature, at least for those who produce it. Literature, in his mind, is connected with the idea of garrets and extreme poverty; and, therefore, having the national respect for money, he in secret, if not in public, despises it. A tree is known by its fruit, says he. Let a man succeed at the Bar, and he makes thousands upon thousands a year, and is promoted to the highest offices in the State. Let a man succeed in art, and he will be paid one or two thousand pounds apiece for his most "pot-boilery" portraits. But your literary men—why, with a few fortunate exceptions, the best of them barely make a living. What can literature be worth, if a man can't make a fortune out of it? So argues the Briton—no doubt with some of his sound common-sense. Not that he has no respect for genius. All men bow to true genius, even when they fear and envy it. But he thinks a good deal more of genius dead than genius living. However this may be, there is no doubt but that if through any cause—such, for instance, as the sudden discovery by the great and highly civilised American people that the seventh commandment was probably intended to apply to authors, amongst the rest of the world—the pecuniary rewards of literary labor should be put more upon an equality with those of other trades, literature—as a profession—will go up many steps in popular esteem. At present, if a member of a family has betaken himself to the high and honourable calling (for surely, it is both) of letters, his friends and relations are apt to talk about him in a shy and diffident, not to say apologetic, way; much as they would had he adopted another sort of book-making as a means of livelihood.

Thus it was that, notwithstanding her success, Augusta had nowhere to turn in her difficulty. She had absolutely no literary connection. Nobody had called upon her, and sought her out in consequence of her book. One or two authors in London, and a few unknown people from different parts of the country and abroad, had written to her—that was all. Had she lived in town it might have been different; but, unfortunately for her, she did not.

The more she thought, the less clear did her path become; until, at last, she got an inspiration. Why not leave England altogether? She had nothing to keep her here. She had a cousin—a clergyman—in New Zealand, whom she had never seen, but who had read "Jemima's Vow," and written her a kind letter about it. That was the one delightful thing about writing books; one made friends all over the world. Surely he would take her in for a while, and put her in the way of earning a living where Meeson would not be to molest her? Why should she not go? She had twenty pounds left, and the furniture (which included an expensive invalid chair), and books would fetch another thirty or so—enough to pay for a second-class passage and leave a few pounds in her pocket. At the worst it would be a change, and she could not go through more there than she did here, so that very night she sat down and wrote to her clergyman cousin.

CHAPTER V.
THE R.M.S. KANGAROO.

It was on a Tuesday evening that a mighty vessel was steaming majestically out of the mouth of the Thames, and shaping her imposing course straight at the ball of the setting sun. Most people will remember reading descriptions of the steamship Kangaroo, and being astonished at the power of her engines, the beauty of her fittings, and the extraordinary speed—about eighteen knots—which she developed in her trials, with an unusually low expenditure of coal. For the benefit of those who have not, however, it may be stated that the Kangaroo, "the Little Kangaroo," as she was ironically named among sailor men, was the very latest development of the science of modern ship-building. Everything about her, from the electric light and boiler tubes up, was on a new and patent system.

Four hundred feet and more she measured from stem to stern, and in that space were crowded and packed all the luxuries of a palace, and all the conveniences of an American hotel. She was a beautiful and a wonderful thing to look on; as, with her holds full of costly merchandise and her decks crowded with her living freight of about a thousand human beings, she steamed slowly out to sea, as though loth to leave the land where she was born. But presently she seemed to gather up her energies and to grow conscious of the thousands and thousands of miles of wide tossing water, which stretched between her and the far-off harbour where her mighty heart should cease from beating and be for a while at rest. Quicker and quicker she sped along, and spurned the churning water from her swift sides. She was running under a full head of steam now, and the coast-line of England grew faint and low in the faint, low light, till at last it almost vanished from the gaze of a tall, slim girl, who stood forward, clinging to the starboard bulwark netting and looking with deep grey eyes across the waste of waters. Presently Augusta, for it was she, could see the shore no more, and turned to watch the other passengers and think. She was sad at heart, poor girl, and felt what she was—a very waif upon the sea of life. Not that she had much to regret upon the vanished coast-line. A little grave with a white cross over it—that was all. She had left no friends to weep for her, none. But even as she thought it, a recollection rose up in her mind of Eustace Meeson's pleasant, handsome face, and of his kind words, and with it came a pang as she reflected that, in all probability, she should never see the one or hear the other again. Why, she wondered, had he not come to see her again? She should have liked to bid him "Good-bye," and had half a mind to send him a note and tell him of her going. This, on second thoughts, however, she had decided not to do; for one thing, she did not know his address, and—well, there was an end of it.

Could she by the means of clairvoyance have seen Eustace's face and heard his words, she would have regretted her decision. For even as that great vessel plunged on her fierce way right into the heart of the gathering darkness, he was standing at the door of the lodging-house in the little street in Birmingham.

"Gone!" he was saying. "Miss Smithers gone to New Zealand! What is her address?"

"She didn't leave no address, sir," replies the dirty maid-of-all-work with a grin. "She went from here two days ago, and was going on to the ship in London."

"What was the name of the ship?" he asked, in despair. "Kan—Kon—Conger-eel," replies the girl in triumph, and shuts the door in his face.

Poor Eustace! He had gone to London to try and get some employment, and having, after some difficulty, succeeded in obtaining a billet as reader in Latin, French and English to a publishing house of good repute, at a salary of £180 a year, he had hurried back to Birmingham for the sole purpose of seeing Miss Augusta Smithers, with whom, if the whole truth must be told, he had, to his credit be it said, fallen deeply, truly, and violently in love. Indeed, so far was he in this way gone, that he had determined to make all the progress that he could, and if he thought that there was any prospect of success, to declare his passion. This was, perhaps, a little premature; but then in these matters people are apt to be more premature than is generally supposed. Human nature is very swift in coming to conclusions in matters in which that strange mixture we call the affections are involved; perhaps because, although the conclusion is not altogether a pleasing one, the affections, at any rate in the beginning, are largely dependent on the senses.

Pity a poor young man! To come from London to Birmingham to woo one's grey-eyed mistress, in a third-class carriage too, and find her gone to New Zealand, whither circumstances prevented him from following her, without leaving a word or a line, or even an address behind her! It was too bad. Well, there was no remedy in the matter; so he walked to the railway station, and groaned and swore all the way back to London.

Augusta, on board the Kangaroo, was, however, in utter ignorance of this act of devotion on the part of her admirer; indeed, she did not even know that he was her admirer. Feeling a curious sinking sensation within her, she was about to go below to her cabin, which she shared with a lady's-maid, not knowing whether to attribute it to sentimental qualms incidental to her lonely departure from the land of her birth, or to other qualms connected with the first experience of life upon the ocean wave. About that moment, however, a burly quarter-master addressed her in gruff tones, and informed her that if she wanted to see the last of "hold Halbion," she had better go aft a bit, and look over the port side, and she would see the something or other light. Accordingly, more to prove to herself that she was not sea-sick than for any other reason, she did so, and, standing as far aft as the second-class passengers were allowed to go, stared at the quick flashes of the light-house, as second by second, they sent their message across the great waste of sea.

As she stood there, holding on to a stanchion to steady herself, for the vessel, large as she was, had begun to get a bit of a roll on, she was suddenly aware of a bulky figure of a man which came running or rather reeling against the bulwarks alongside of her, where it—or rather he—was instantly and violently ill. Augusta was, not unnaturally, almost horrified into following the figure's example, when, suddenly growing faint or from some other cause, it loosed its hold and rolled into the scuppers, where it lay feebly swearing. Augusta, obeying a tender impulse of humanity, hurried forward and stretched out the hand of succour, and presently, between her help and that of the bulwark netting, the man struggled to his feet. As he did so his face came close to hers, and in the dim light she recognised the fat, coarse features, now blanched with misery, of Mr. Meeson, the publisher. There was no doubt about it, it was her enemy; the man whose behavior had indirectly, as she believed, caused the death of her little sister. She dropped his hand with an exclamation of disgust and dismay, and as she did so he recognised who she was.

"Hullo!" he said, with a faint and rather feeble attempt to assume his fine old crusted publishing-company manners. "Hullo! Miss Jemima—Smithers, I mean; what on earth are you doing here?"

"I am going to New Zealand, Mr. Meeson," she answered sharply; "and I certainly did not expect to have the pleasure of your company on the voyage."

"Going to New Zealand," he said, "are you? Why, so am I; at least, I am going there first, then to Australia. What do you mean to do there—try and run round our little agreement, eh? It won't be any good, I tell you plainly. We have our agents in New Zealand, and a house in Australia, and if you try to get the better of Meeson's there, Meeson's will be even with you, Miss Smithers—Oh, Heavens! I feel as though I were coming to pieces."

"Don't alarm yourself, Mr. Meeson," she answered, "I am not going to publish any more books at present."

"That is a pity," he said, "because your stuff is good selling stuff. Any publisher would find money in it. I suppose you are second-class, Miss Smithers, so we shan't see much of each other; and, perhaps, if we should meet, it might be as well if we didn't seem to have any acquaintance. It don't look well for a man in my position to know second-class passengers, especially young lady passengers who write novels."

"You need not be afraid, Mr. Meeson: I have no wish to claim your acquaintance," said Augusta.

At this point, her enemy was taken violently worse again, and, being unable to stand the sight and sound of his writhing and groaning, she fled forward; and, reflecting on this strange and awkward meeting, went down to her own berth, where, with lucid intervals, she remained helpless and half stupid for the next three days. On the fourth day, however, she reappeared on deck quite recovered, and with an excellent appetite. She had her breakfast, and then went and sat forward in as quiet a place as she could find. She did not want to see Mr. Meeson any more, and she did want to escape from the stories of her cabin-mate, the lady's-maid. This good person would, after the manner of her kind, insist upon repeating to her a succession of histories connected with members of the families with whom she had lived, many of which were sufficient to make the hair of a respectable young lady like Augusta stand positively on end. No doubt they were interesting to her in her capacity of a novelist; but, as they were all of the same colour, and as their tendency was absolutely to destroy any belief she might have in virtue as an inherent quality in highly developed woman or honour in man, Augusta soon wearied of these *chroniques scandaleuses*. So she went forward, and was sitting looking at the "white horses" chasing each other across the watery plain, and reflecting upon what the condition of mind of those ladies whose histories she had recently heard would be if they knew that their most secret, and in some cases disgraceful and tragic, love affairs were the common talk of a dozen servants' halls, when suddenly she was astonished by the appearance of a splendid official bearing a book. At first, from the quantity of gold lace with which his uniform was adorned, Augusta took him to be the captain; but it presently transpired that he was only the chief steward.

"Please, Miss," he said, touching his hat and holding out the book in his hand towards her, "the captain sends his compliments and wants to know if you are the young lady who wrote this."

Augusta glanced at the work. It was a copy of "Jemima's Vow." Then she replied that she was the writer of it, and the steward vanished.

Later on in the morning came another surprise. The gorgeous official again appeared, touched his cap, and said that the captain desired him to say that orders had been given to have her things moved to a cabin further aft. At first Augusta demurred to this, not from any love of the lady's-maid, but because she had a truly British objection to being ordered about.

"Captain's orders, Miss," said the man, touching his cap again; and she yielded.

Nor had she any cause to regret doing so; for, to her huge delight, she found herself moved into a charming deck-cabin on the starboard side of the vessel, some little way abaft the engine-room. It was evidently an officer's cabin, for there, over the head of the bed, was the picture of a young lady he adored, and also some neatly fitted shelves of books, a rack of telescopes, and other seaman-like contrivances.

"Am I to have this cabin to myself?" asked Augusta of the steward.

"Yes, Miss; those are the captain's orders. It is Mr. Jones's cabin. Mr. Jones is the second officer; but he has turned in with Mr. Thomas, the first officer, and given up the cabin to you."

"I am sure it's very kind of Mr. Jones," murmured Augusta, not knowing what to make of this turn of fortune. But surprises were not to end there. A few minutes afterwards, just as she was leaving the cabin, a gentleman in uniform came up, in whom she recognized the captain. He was accompanied by a pretty fair-haired woman very becomingly dressed.

"Excuse me; Miss Smithers, I believe?" he said, with a bow.

"Yes."

"I am Captain Alton. I hope you like your new cabin. Let me introduce you to Lady Holmhurst, wife of Lord Holmhurst, the New Zealand Governor, you know. Lady Holmhurst, this is Miss Smithers, whose book you were talking so much about."

"Oh! I am delighted to make your acquaintance, Miss Smithers," said the great lady in a manner that evidently was not assumed. "Captain Alton has promised that I shall sit next to you at dinner, and then we can have a good talk. I don't know when I have been so much delighted with anything as I was with your book. I have read it three times, what do you think of that for a busy woman?"

"I think there is some mistake," said Augusta, hurriedly and with a slight blush. "I am a second-class passenger on board this ship, and therefore cannot have the pleasure of sitting next to Lady Holmhurst."

"Oh, that is all right, Miss Smithers," said the captain, with a jolly laugh. "You are my guest, and I shall take no denial."

"When we find genius for once in our lives, we are not going to lose the opportunity of sitting at its feet," added Lady Holmhurst, with a little movement towards her which was neither curtsey nor bow, but rather a happy combination of both. The compliment was, Augusta felt, sincere, however much it exaggerated the measure of her poor capacities, and, putting other things aside, was, coming as it did from one woman to another, peculiarly graceful and surprising. She blushed and bowed, scarcely knowing what to say, when suddenly, Mr. Meeson's harsh tones, pitched just now in a respectful key, broke upon her ear. Mr. Meeson was addressing no less a person than Lord Holmhurst, G.C.M.G. Lord Holmhurst was a stout, short, dark little man, with a somewhat pompous manner, and a kindly face. He was a Colonial Governor of the first water, and was perfectly aware of the fact.

Now, a Colonial Governor, even though he be a G.C.M.G. when he is at home, is not a name to conjure with, and does not fill an exclusive place in the eye of the English world. There are many Colonial Governors in the present and past tense to be found in the purlieus of South Kensington, where their presence creates no unusual excitement. But when one of this honourable corps sets foot upon the vessel destined to bear him to the shores that he shall rule, all this changes. He puts off the body of the ordinary betitled individual and puts on the body of the celestial brotherhood. In short, from being nobody out of the common he becomes, and very properly so, a great man. Nobody knew this better than Lord Holmhurst, and to a person fond of observing such things nothing could have been more curious to notice than the small, but gradual increase of the pomposity of his manner, as the great ship day by day steamed further from England and nearer to the country where he was King. It went up, degree by degree, like a thermometer which is taken down into the bowels of the earth or gradually removed into the sunlight. At present, however, the thermometer was only rising.

"I was repeating, my Lord," said the harsh voice of Mr. Meeson, "that the principle of an hereditary peerage is the grandest principle our country has yet developed. It gives us something to look forward to. In one generation we make the money; in the next we take the title which the money buys. Look at your Lordship. Your Lordship is now in a proud position; but, as I have understood, your Lordship's father was a trader like me."

"Hum!—well, not exactly, Mr. Meeson," broke in Lord Holmhurst. "Dear me, I wonder who that exceedingly nice-looking girl Lady Holmhurst is talking to can be!"

"Now, your Lordship, to put a case," went on the remorseless Meeson, who, like most people of his stamp, had an almost superstitious veneration for the aristocracy, "I have made a great deal of money, as I do not mind telling your Lordship; what is there to prevent my successor—supposing I have a successor—from taking advantage of that money, and rising on it to a similar position to that so worthily occupied by your Lordship?"

"Exactly, Mr. Meeson. A most excellent idea for your successor. Excuse me, but I see Lady Holmhurst beckoning to me." And he fled precipitately, still followed by Mr. Meeson.

"John, my dear!" said Lady Holmhurst, "I want to introduce you to Miss Smithers—*the* Miss Smithers whom we have all been talking about, and whose book you have been reading. Miss Smithers, my husband!"

Lord Holmhurst, who, when he was not deep in the affairs of State, had a considerable eye for a pretty girl—and what man worthy of the name has not?—bowed most politely, and was proceeding to tell Augusta, in very charming language, how delighted he was to make her acquaintance, when Mr. Meeson arrived on the scene and perceived Augusta for the first time. Quite taken aback at finding her, apparently, upon the very best of terms with people of such quality, he hesitated to consider what course to adopt; whereon Lady Holmhurst in a somewhat formal way, for she was not very fond of Mr. Meeson, mistaking his hesitation, went on to introduce him. Thereupon, all in a moment, as we do sometimes take such resolutions, Augusta came to a determination. She would have nothing more to do with Mr. Meeson—she would repudiate him then and there, come what would of it.

So, as he advanced upon her with outstretched hand, she drew herself up, and in a cold and determined voice said, "I already know Mr. Meeson, Lady Holmhurst; and I do not wish to have anything more to do with him. Mr. Meeson has not behaved well to me."

"'Pon my word," murmured Lord Holmhurst to himself, "I don't wonder she has had enough of him. Sensible young woman, that!"

Lady Holmhurst looked a little astonished and a little amused. Suddenly, however, a light broke upon her.

"Oh! I see," she said. "I suppose that Mr. Meeson published 'Jemima's Vow.' Of course that accounts for it. Why, I declare there is the dinner bell! Come along, Miss Smithers, or we shall lose the place the captain has promised us." And, accordingly, they went, leaving Mr. Meeson, who had not yet realized the unprecedented nature of the position, positively gasping on the deck. And on board the Kangaroo there were no clerks and editors on whom he could wreak his wrath!

"And now, my dear Miss Smithers," said Lady Holmhurst when, dinner being over, they were sitting together in the moonlight, near the wheel, "perhaps you will tell me why you don't like Mr. Meeson, whom, by-the-way, I personally detest. But don't, if you don't wish to, you know."

But Augusta did wish to, and then and there she unfolded her whole sad story into her new-found friend's sympathetic ear; and glad enough the poor girl was to find a confidante to whom she could unbosom her sorrows.

"Well, upon my word!" said Lady Holmhurst, when she had listened with tears in her eyes to the history of poor little Jeannie's death, "upon my word, of all the brutes I ever heard of, I think that this publisher of yours is the worst! I will cut him, and get my husband to cut him too. But no, I have a better plan than that. He shall tear up that agreement, so sure as my name is Bessie Holmhurst; he shall tear it up, or—or"—and she nodded her little head with an air of infinite wisdom.

CHAPTER VI.
MR. TOMBEY GOES FORWARD.

From that day forward, the voyage on the Kangaroo was, until the last dread catastrophe, a very happy one for Augusta. Lord and Lady Holmhurst made much of her, and all the rest of the first-class passengers followed suit, and soon she found herself the most popular character on board. The two copies of her book that there were on the ship were passed on from hand to hand till they would hardly hang together, and, really, at last she got quite tired of hearing of her own creations. But this was not all; Augusta was, it will be remembered, an exceedingly pretty woman, and melancholy as the fact may seem, it still remains a fact that a pretty woman is in the eyes of most people a more interesting object than a man, or than a lady, who is not "built that way." Thus it came to pass that what between her youth, her beauty, her talent, and her misfortunes—for Lady Holmhurst had not exactly kept that history to herself—Augusta was all of a sudden elevated into the position of a perfect heroine. It really almost frightened the poor girl, who had been accustomed to nothing but sorrow, ill-treatment and grinding poverty, to suddenly find herself in this strange position, with every man on board that great vessel at her beck and call. But she was human, and therefore, of course she enjoyed it. It *is* something when one has been wandering for hour after hour in the wet and melancholy night, suddenly to see the fair dawn breaking and burning overhead, and to know that the worst is over, for now there will be light whereby to set our feet. It is something, too, to the most Christian soul, to utterly and completely triumph over one who had done all in his power to crush and destroy you; whose grasping greed has indirectly been the cause of the death of the person you loved best in the whole world round. And she did triumph. As Mr. Meeson's conduct to her got about, the little society of the ship—which was, after all, a very fair example of all society in miniature—fell away from this publishing Prince, and not even the jingling of his money-bags could lure it back. He the great, the practically omnipotent, the owner of two millions, and the hard master of hundreds upon whose toil he battened, was practically *cut*. Even the clerk, who was going out on a chance of getting a place in a New Zealand bank, would have nothing to say to him. And what is more, he felt it more even than an ordinary individual would have done. He, the "Printer-devil," as poor little Jeannie used to call him, he to be slighted and flouted by a pack of people whom he could buy up three times over, and all on account of a wretched authoress—an authoress, if you please! It made Mr. Meeson very wild—a state of affairs which was brought to a climax when one morning Lord Holmhurst, who had for several days been showing a growing dislike to his society, actually almost cut him dead; that is, he did not notice his outstretched hand, and passed him with a slight bow.

"Never mind, my Lord—never mind!" muttered Mr. Meeson after that somewhat pompous but amiable nobleman's retreating form. "We'll see if I can't come square with you. I'm a dog who can pull a string or two in the English press, I am! Those who have the money and have got a hold of people, so that they must write what they tell them, ain't people to be cut by any Colonial Governor, my Lord!" And in his anger he fairly shook his fist at the unconscious Peer.

"Seem to be a little out of temper, Mr. Meeson," said a voice at his elbow, the owner of which was a big young man with hard but kindly features and a large moustache. "What has the Governor been doing to you?"

"Doing, Mr. Tombey? He's been cutting me, that's all—me, Meeson!—cutting me as dead as offal, or something like it. I held out my hand and he looked right over it, and marched by."

"Ah!" said Mr. Tombey, who was a wealthy New Zealand landowner; "and now, why do you suppose he did that?"

"Why? I'll tell you why. It's all about that girl."

"Miss Smithers, do you mean?" said Tombey the big, with a curious flash of his deep-set eyes.

"Yes, Miss Smithers. She wrote a book, and I bought the book for fifty pounds, and stuck a clause in that she should give me the right to publish anything she wrote for five years at a price—a common sort of thing enough in one way and another, when you are dealing with some idiot who don't know any better. Well, as it happened this book sold like wild-fire; and, in time the young lady comes to me and wants more money, wants to get out of the hanging clause in the agreement, wants everything, like a female Oliver Twist; and when I say, 'No, you don't,' loses her temper, and makes a scene. And it turns out that what she wanted the money for was to take a sick sister, or cousin, or aunt, or someone, out of England; and when she could not do it, and the relation died, then she emigrates, and goes and tells the people on board ship that it is all my fault."

"And I suppose that that is a conclusion that you do not feel drawn to, Mr. Meeson?"

"No Tombey, I don't. Business is business; and if I happen to have got to windward of the young woman, why, so much the better for me. She's getting her experience, that's all; and she ain't the first, and won't be the last. But if she goes saying much more about me, I go for her for slander, that's sure."

"On the legal ground that the greater the truth, the greater the libel, I presume?"

"Confound her!" went on Meeson, without noticing his remark, and contracting his heavy eyebrows, "there's no end to the trouble she has brought on me. I quarrelled with my nephew about her, and now she's dragging my name through the dirt here, and I'll bet the story will go all over New Zealand and Australia."

"Yes," said Mr. Tombey, "I fancy you will find it take a lot of choking; and now, Mr. Meeson, with your permission I will say a word, and try and throw a new light upon a very perplexing matter. It never seems to have occurred to you what an out-and-out blackguard you are, so I may as well put it to you plainly. If you are not a thief, you are, at least, a very well-coloured imitation. You take a girl's book and make hundreds upon hundreds out of it, and give her fifty. You tie her down, so as to provide for successful swindling of the same sort, during future years, and then, when she comes to beg a few pounds of you, you show her the door. And now you wonder, Mr. Meeson, that respectable people will have nothing to do with you! Well, now, I tell you, *my* opinion is that the only society to which you would be really suited is that of cow-hide. Good morning," and the large young man walked off, his very moustachios curling with wrath and contempt. Thus, for a second time, did the great Mr. Meeson hear the truth from the lips of babes and sucklings, and the worst of it was that he could not disinherit Number Two as he had Number One.

Now this will strike the reader as being very warm advocacy on the part of Mr. Tombey, who, being called in to console and bless, cursed with such extraordinary vigour. It may even strike the discerning reader—and all readers, or, at least, nearly all readers, are of course discerning: far too much so, indeed—that there must have been a reason for it; and the discerning reader will be right. Augusta's grey eyes had been too much for Mr. Tombey, as they had been too much for Eustace Meeson before him. His passion had sprung up and ripened in that peculiarly rapid and vigorous fashion that passions do on board ship. A passenger steamer is Cupid's own hot-bed, and in this way differs from a sailing-ship. On the sailing-ship, indeed, the preliminary stages are the same. The seed roots as strongly, and grows and flowers with equal vigour; but here comes the melancholy part—it withers and decays with equal rapidity. The voyage is too long. Too much is mutually revealed. The matrimonial iron cannot be struck while it is hot, and long before the weary ninety days are over it is once more cold and black, or at the best glows with but a feeble heat. But on the steamship there is no time for this, as any traveller knows. Myself—I, the historian—have, with my own eyes seen a couple meet for the first time at Maderia, get married at the Cape, and go on as man and wife in the same vessel to Natal. And, therefore, it came to pass that very evening a touching, and, on the whole melancholy, little scene was enacted near the smoke-stack of the Kangaroo.

Mr. Tombey and Miss Augusta Smithers were leaning together over the bulwarks and watching the phosphorescent foam go flashing past. Mr. Tombey was nervous and ill at ease; Miss Smithers very much at ease, and reflecting that her companion's moustachios would very well become a villain in a novel.

Mr. Tombey looked at the star-spangled sky, on which the Southern Cross hung low, and he looked at the phosphorescent sea; but from neither did inspiration come. Inspiration is from within, and not from without. At last, however, he made a gallant and a desperate effort.

"Miss Smithers," he said in a voice trembling with agitation.

"Yes, Mr. Tombey," answered Augusta, quietly; "what is it?"

"Miss Smithers," he went on—"Miss Augusta, I don't know what you will think of me, but I must tell you, I can't keep it any longer, I love you!"

Augusta fairly jumped. Mr. Tombey had been very, even markedly, polite, and she, not being a fool, had seen that he admired her; but she had never expected this, and the suddenness with which the shot was fired was somewhat bewildering.

"Why, Mr. Tombey," she said in a surprised voice, "you have only known me for a little more than a fortnight."

"I fell in love with you when I had only known you for an hour," he answered with evident sincerity. "Please listen to me. I know I am not worthy of you! But I do love you so very dearly, and I would make you a good husband; indeed I would, I am well off; though, of course that is nothing; and if you don't like New Zealand, I would give it up and go to live in England. Do you think that you can take me? If you only knew how dearly I love you, I am sure you would."

Augusta collected her wits as well as she could. The man evidently did love her; there was no doubting the sincerity of his words, and she liked him and he was a gentleman. If she married him there would be an end of all her worries and troubles, and she could rest contentedly on his strong arm. Woman, even gifted woman, is not made to fight the world with her own hand, and the prospect had allurements. But while she thought, Eustace Meeson's bonny face rose before her eyes, and, as it did so, a faint feeling of repulsion to the man who was pleading with her took form and colour in her breast. Eustace Meeson, of course, was nothing to her; no word or sign of affection had passed between them; and the probability was that she would never set her eyes upon him again. And yet that face rose up between her and this man who was pleading at her side. Many women, likely enough, have seen some such vision from the past and have disregarded it, only to find too late that that which is thrust aside is not necessarily hidden; for alas! those faces of our departed youth have an uncanny trick of rising from the tomb of our forgetfulness. But Augusta was not of the great order of opportunists. Because a thing might be convenient, it did not, according to the dictates of her moral sense, follow that it was lawful. Therefore, she was a woman to be respected. For a woman who, except under most exceptional circumstances, gives her instincts the lie in order to pander to her convenience or her desire for wealth and social ease, is not altogether a woman to be respected.

In a very few seconds she had made up her mind.

"I am very much obliged to you, Mr. Tombey," she said; "you have done me a great honour, the greatest honour man can do to a woman; but I cannot marry you."

"Are you sure?" gasped the unfortunate Tombey, for his hopes had been high. "Is there no hope for me? Perhaps there is somebody else!"

"There is nobody else, Mr. Tombey; and, I am sorry to say, you don't know how much it pains me to say it, I cannot hold out any prospect that I shall change my mind."

He dropped his head upon his hands for a minute, and then lifted it again.

"Very well," he said slowly; "it can't be helped. I never loved any woman before, and I never shall again. It is a pity "—(with a hard, little laugh)—"that so much first-class affection should be wasted. But, there you are; it is all part and parcel of the pleasant experiences which make up our lives. Good-bye, Miss Smithers; at least, good-bye as a friend!"

"We can still be friends," she faltered.

"Oh, no," he answered, with another laugh; "that is an exploded notion. Friendship of that nature is not very safe under any circumstances, certainly not under these. The relationship is antagonistic to the facts of life, and the friends, or one or other of them, will drift either into indifference and dislike, or—something warmer. You are a novelist, Miss Smithers; perhaps some day you will write a book to explain why people fall in love where their affection is not wanted, and what purpose their distress can possibly serve. And now, once more, good bye!" and he lifted her hand to his lips and gently kissed it, and then, with a bow, turned and went.

From all of which it will be clearly seen that Mr. Tombey was decidedly a young man above the average, and one who took punishment very well. Augusta looked after him, and sighed deeply, and even wiped away a tear. Then she turned and walked aft, to where Lady Holmhurst was sitting enjoying the balmy southern air, through which the great ship was rushing with outspread sails like some huge white bird, and chatting to the captain.

As she came up, the captain made his bow and departed, saying that he had something to see to, and for a minute Lady Holmhurst and Augusta were left alone.

"Well, Augusta?" said Lady Holmhurst, for she called her "Augusta" now. "And what have you done with that young man, Mr. Tombey—that very nice young man?" she added with emphasis.

"I think that Mr. Tombey went forward," said Augusta.

The two women looked at each other, and, womanlike, each understood what the other meant. Lady Holmhurst had not been altogether innocent in the Tombey affair.

"Lady Holmhurst," said Augusta, taking the bull by the horns, "Mr. Tombey has been speaking to me and has"—

"Proposed to you," suggested Lady Holmhurst, admiring the Southern Cross through her eyeglasses. "You said he went forward, you know."

"Has proposed to me," answered Augusta, ignoring the little joke. "I regret," she went on hurriedly, "that I have not been able to fall in with Mr. Tombey's plans."

"Ah!" said Lady Holmhurst; "I am sorry, for some things. Mr. Tombey is such a very nice young man, and so very gentlemanlike. I thought that perhaps it might suit your views, and it would have simplified your future arrangements. But as to that, of course, while you are in New Zealand, I shall be able to see to that. By-the-way, it is understood that you come to stay with us for a few months at Government House, before you hunt up your cousin."

"You are very good to me, Lady Holmhurst," said Augusta, with something like a sob.

"Suppose, my dear," answered the great lady, laying her little hand upon Augusta's beautiful hair, "that you were to drop the 'Lady Holmhurst' and call me 'Bessie?' it sounds so much more sociable, you know, and, besides; it is shorter, and does not waste so much breath."

Then Augusta sobbed outright, for her nerves were shaken: "You don't know what your kindness means to me," she said; "I have never had a friend, and since my darling died I have been so very lonely!"

CHAPTER VII.
THE CATASTROPHE.

And so these two fair women talked, making plans for the future as though all things endured forever, and all plans were destined to be realized. But even as they talked, somewhere up in the high heavens the Voice that rules the world spoke a word, and the Messenger of Fate rushed forth to do its bidding. On board the great ship was music and laughter and the sweet voices of singing women; but above it hung a pall of doom. Not the most timid heart dreamed of danger. What danger could there be aboard of that grand ship, which sped across the waves with the lightness and confidence of the swallow? There was naught to fear. A prosperous voyage was drawing to its end, and mothers put their babes to sleep with as sure a heart as though they were on solid English ground. Oh! surely when his overflowing load of sorrows and dire miseries was meted out to man, some gentle Spirit pleaded for him—that he should not have foresight added to the tale, that he should not see the falling knife or hear the water lapping that one day shall entomb him? Or, was it kept back because man, having knowledge, would be man without reason?—for terror would make him mad, and he would end his fears by hurrying their fulfilment! At least, we are blind to the future, and let us be thankful for it.

Presently Lady Holmhurst got up from her chair, and said that she was going to bed, but that, first of all, she must kiss Dick, her little boy, who slept with his nurse in another cabin. Augusta rose and went with her, and they both kissed the sleeping child, a bonny boy of five, and then they kissed each other and separated for the night.

Some hours afterwards Augusta woke up, feeling very restless. For an hour or more she lay thinking of Mr. Tombey and many other things, and listening to the swift "lap, lap," of the water as it slipped past the vessel's sides, and the occasional tramp of the watch as they set fresh sails. At last her feeling of unrest got too much for her, and she rose and partially, very partially, dressed herself—for in the gloom she could only find her flannel vest and petticoat—twisted her long hair in a coil round her head, put on a hat and a thick ulster that hung upon the door—for they were running into chilly latitudes—and slipped out on deck.

It was getting towards dawn, but the night was still dark. Looking up, Augusta could only just make out the outlines of the huge bellying sails, for the Kangaroo was rushing along before the westerly wind under a full head of steam, and with every inch of her canvas set to ease the screw. There was something very exhilarating about the movement, the freshness of the night, and the wild, sweet song of the wind as it sang amongst the rigging. Augusta turned her face toward it, and, being alone, stretched out her arms as though to catch it. The whole scene awoke some answering greatness in her heart; something that slumbers in the bosom of the higher race of human beings, and only stirs—and then but faintly—when the passions move them, or when nature communes with her nobler children. She felt that at that moment she could write as she had never written yet. All sorts of beautiful ideas, all sorts of aspirations after that noble calm, and purity of thought and life for which we pray and long, but are not allowed to reach, came flowing into her heart. She almost thought that she could hear her lost Jeannie's voice calling down the gale, and her strong imagination began to paint her hovering like a sea-bird upon white wings high above the mainmast's taper point, and gazing through the darkness into the soul of her she loved. Then, by those faint and imperceptible degrees with which thoughts fade one into another, from Jeannie her thought got round to Eustace Meeson. She wondered if he had ever called at the lodgings at Birmingham after she left? Somehow, she had an idea that he was not altogether indifferent to her; there had been a look in his eyes she did not quite understand. She almost wished now she had sent him a line or a message. Perhaps she would do so from New Zealand. Just then her meditations were interrupted by a step, and, turning round, she found herself face to face with the captain.

"Why, Miss Smithers!" he said, "what on earth are you doing here at this hour?—making up romances?"

"Yes," she answered, laughing, and with perfect truth. "The fact of the matter is, I could not sleep, and so I came on deck; and very pleasant it is!"

"Yes," said the captain, "If you want something to put into your stories you won't find anything better than this. The Kangaroo is showing her heels, isn't she, Miss Smithers? That's the beauty of her, she can sail as well as steam; and when she has a strong wind like this abaft, it would have to be something very quick that would catch her. I believe that we have been running over seventeen knots an hour ever since midnight. I hope to make Kerguelen Island by seven o'clock to correct my chronometers."

"What is Kerguelen Island?" asked Augusta.

"Oh! it is a desert place where nobody goes, except now and then a whaler to fill up with water. I believe that the astronomers sent an expedition there a few years ago, to observe the transit of Venus: but it was a failure because the weather was so misty—it is nearly always misty there. Well, I must be off, Miss Smithers. Good night; or, rather, good morning."

Before the words were well out of his mouth, there was a wild shout forward—"*ship ahead*!" Then came an awful yell from a dozen voices—"*starboard! Hard-a-starboard, for God's sake.*"

With a wild leap, like the leap of a man suddenly shot, the captain left her side and rushed on to the bridge. At the same instant the engine-bell rang and the steering-chains began to rattle furiously on the rollers at her feet as the steam steering-gear did its work. Then came another yell—

"*It's a whaler!—no lights!*" and an answering shriek of terror from some big black object that loomed ahead. Before the echoes had died away, before the great ship could even answer to her helm, there was a crash, such as Augusta had never heard, and a sickening shock, that threw her on her hands and knees on the deck, shaking the iron masts till they trembled as though they were willow wands, and making the huge sails flap and for an instant fly aback. The great vessel, rushing along at her frightful speed of seventeen knots, had plunged into the ship ahead with such hideous energy that she cut her clean in two—cut her in two and passed over her, as though she were a pleasure-boat!

Shriek upon shriek of despair came piercing the gloomy night, and then, as Augusta struggled to her feet, she felt a horrible succession of bumps, accompanied by a crushing, grinding noise. It was the Kangaroo driving right over the remains of the whaler.

In a very few seconds it was done, and looking astern, Augusta could just make out something black that seemed to float for a second or two upon the water, and then disappear into its depths. It was the shattered hull of the whaler.

Then there arose a faint murmuring sound, that grew first into a hum, then into a roar, and then into a clamour that rent the skies, and up from every hatchway and cabin in the great ship, human beings—men, women, and children—came rushing and tumbling, with faces white with terror—white as their night-gear. Some were absolutely naked, having slipped off their night-dress and had no time to put on anything else; some had put on ulsters and great-coats, others had blankets thrown round them or carried their clothes in their hands. Up they came, hundreds and hundreds of them (for there were a thousand souls on board the Kangaroo), pouring aft like terrified spirits flying from the mouth of Hell, and from them arose such a hideous clamour as few have lived to hear.

Augusta clung to the nettings to let the rush go by, trying to collect her scattered senses and to prevent herself from catching the dreadful contagion of the panic. Being a brave and cool-headed woman, she presently succeeded, and with her returning clearness of vision she realized that she and all on board were in great peril. It was clear that so frightful a collision could not have taken place without injury to their own vessel. Nothing short of an iron-clad ram could have stood such a shock, probably they would founder in a few minutes, and all be drowned. In a few minutes she might be dead! Her heart stood still at the horror of the thought, but once more she recovered herself. Well, after all, life had not been pleasant; and she had nothing to fear from another world, she had done no wrong. Then suddenly she began to think of the others. Where was Lady Holmhurst? and where were the boy and the nurse? Acting upon the impulse she did not stay to realize, she ran to the saloon hatchway. It was fairly clear now, for most of the people were on deck, and she found her way to the child's cabin with but little difficulty. There was a light in it, and the first glance showed her that the nurse had gone; gone, and deserted the child—for there he lay, asleep, with a smile upon his little round face. The shock had scarcely wakened the boy, and, knowing nothing of ship-wrecks, he had just shut his eyes and gone to sleep again.

"Dick, Dick!" she said, shaking him.

He yawned and sat up, and then threw himself down again saying, "Dick sleepy."

"Yes, but Dick must wake up, and Auntie" (he called her "auntie") "will take him up on deck to look for Mummy. Won't it be nice to go on deck in the dark."

"Yes," said Dick, with confidence; and Augusta took him on her knee and hurried him into such of his clothes as came handy, as quickly as she could. On the cabin-door was a warm little pea-jacket which the child wore when it was cold. This she put on over his blouse and flannel shirt, and then, by an after-thought, took the two blankets off his bunk and wrapped them round him. At the foot of the nurse's bed was a box of biscuits and some milk. The biscuits she emptied into the pockets of her ulster, and having given the child as much of the milk as he would drink, swallowed the rest herself. Then, pinning a shawl which lay about round her own shoulders, she took up the child and made her way with him on to the deck. At the head of the companion she met Lord Holmhurst himself, rushing down to look after the child.

"I have got him, Lord Holmhurst," she cried; "the nurse has run away. Where is your wife?"

"Bless you," he said fervently; "you are a good girl. Bessie is aft somewhere: I would not let her come. They are trying to keep the people off the boats—they are all mad!"

"Are we sinking?" she asked faintly.

"God knows—ah! here is the captain," pointing to a man who was walking, or rather pushing his way, rapidly towards them through the maddened, screeching mob. Lord Holmhurst caught him by the arm.

"Let me go," he said roughly, trying to shake himself loose. "Oh! it is you, Lord Holmhurst."

"Yes; step in here for one second and tell us the worst. Speak up, man, and let us know all!"

"Very well, Lord Holmhurst, I will. We have run down a whaler of about five hundred tons, which was cruising along under reduced canvas and showing no lights. Our fore compartment is stove right in, bulging out the plates on each side of the cut-water, and loosening the fore bulkhead. The carpenter and his mates are doing their best to shore it up from the inside with balks of timber, but the water is coming in like a mill race, and I fear there are other injuries. All the pumps are at work, but there's a deal of water, and if the bulkhead goes"—

"We shall go, too," said Lord Holmhurst, calmly. "Well, we must take to the boats. Is that all?"

"In Heaven's name, is that not enough!" said the captain, looking up, so that the light that was fixed in the companion threw his ghastly face into bold relief. "No, Lord Holmhurst, it is not all. The boats will hold something over three hundred people. There are about one thousand souls aboard the Kangaroo, of whom more than three hundred are women and children."

"Therefore the men must drown," said Lord Holmhurst, quietly. "God's will be done!"

"Your Lordship will, of course, take a place in the boats?" said the captain, hurriedly. "I have ordered them to be prepared, and, fortunately, day is breaking. I rely upon you to explain matters to the owners if you escape, and clear my character. The boats must make for Kerguelen Land. It is about seventy miles to the eastward."

"You must give your message to someone else, captain," was the answer; "I shall stay and share the fate of the other men."

There was no pomposity about Lord Holmhurst now—all that had gone—and nothing but the simple gallant nature of the English gentleman remained.

"No, no," said the captain, as they hurried aft, pushing their way through the fear-distracted crowd. "Have you got your revolver?"

"Yes."

"Well, then, keep it handy; you may have to use it presently: they will try and rush the boats."

By this time the grey dawn was slowly breaking, throwing a cold and ghastly light upon the hideous scene of terror. Round about the boats were gathered the officers and some of the crew, doing their best to prepare them for lowering. Indeed, one had already been got away. In it was Lady Holmhurst, who had been thrown there against her will, shrieking for her child and husband, and about a score of women and children, together with half-a-dozen sailors and an officer.

Augusta caught sight of her friend's face in the faint light "Bessie! Bessie! Lady Holmhurst!" she cried, "I have got the boy. It is all right—I have got the boy!"

She heard her, and waved her hand wildly towards her; and then the men in the boat gave way, and in a second it was out of earshot. Just then a tall form seized Augusta by the arm. She looked up: it was Mr. Tombey, and she saw that in his other hand he held a revolver.

"Thank God!" he shouted in her ear, "I have found you! This way—this way, quick!" And he dragged her aft to where two sailors, standing by the davits that supported a small boat, were lowering her to the level of the bulwarks.

"Now then, women!" shouted an officer who was in charge of the operation. Some men made a rush.

"Women first! Women first!"

"I am in no hurry," said Augusta, stepping forward with the trembling child in her arms; and her action for a few seconds produced a calming effect, for the men stopped.

"Come on!" said Mr. Tombey, stooping to lift her over the side, only to be nearly knocked down by a man who made a desperate effort to get into the boat. It was Mr. Meeson, and, recognising him, Mr. Tombey dealt him a blow that sent him spinning back.

"A thousand pounds for a place!" he roared. "Ten thousand pounds for a seat in a boat!" And once more he scrambled up at the bulwarks, trampling down a child as he did so, and was once more thrown back.

Mr. Tombey took Augusta and the child into his strong arms and put her into the boat. As he did so, he kissed her forehead and murmured, "God bless you, good-bye!"

At that instant there was a loud report forward, and the stern of the vessel lifted perceptibly. The bulkhead had given way, and there arose such a yell as surely was seldom heard before. To Augusta's ears it seemed to shape itself into the word "*Sinking*!"

Up from the bowels of the ship poured the firemen, the appearance of whose blackened faces, lined with white streaks of perspiration, added a new impulse of terror to the panic-stricken throng. Aft they came, accompanied by a crowd of sailors and emigrants.

"Rush the boats," sung out a voice with a strong Irish accent, "or sure we'll be drowned!"

Taking the hint, the maddened mob burst towards the boats like a flood, blaspheming and shrieking as it came. In a moment the women and children who were waiting to take to the boat, in which Augusta and the two sea-men were already, were swept aside, and a determined effort was made to rush it, headed by a great Irishman, the same who had called out.

Augusta saw Mr. Tombey, Lord Holmhurst, who had come up, and the officer lift their pistols, which exploded almost simultaneously, and the Irishman and another man pitched forward on to their hands and knees.

"Never mind the pistols, lads," shouted a voice; "as well be shot as drown. There isn't room for half of us in the boats; come on!" And a second fearful rush was made, which bore the three gentlemen, firing as they went, right up against the nettings.

"Bill," halloaed the man who was holding on to the foremost tackle, "lower away; we shall be rushed and swamped!"

Bill obeyed with heart and soul, and down sank the boat below the level of the upper decks, just as the mob was getting the mastery. In five seconds more they were hanging close over the water, and whilst they were in this position a man leapt at the boat from the bulwarks. He struck on the thwarts, rolled off into the water, and was no more seen. A lady, the wife of a Colonial Judge, threw her child; Augusta tried to catch it, but missed, and the boy sank and was lost. In another moment the two sailors had shoved off from the ship's side. As they did so, the stern of the Kangaroo lifted right out of the water so that they could see under her rudder-post. Just then, too, with a yell of terror, Mr. Meeson, in whom the elementary principle of self-preservation at all costs was strongly developed, cast himself from the side and fell with a splash within a few feet of the boat. Rising to the surface, he clutched hold of the gunwale, and implored to be taken in.

"Knock the old varmint over the knuckles, Bill," shouted the other man; "he'll upset us!"

"No; no!" cried Augusta, her woman's heart moved at seeing her old enemy in such a case. "There is plenty of room in the boat."

"Hold on then," said the man addressed, whose name was Johnnie; "when we get clear we'll haul you in."

And, the reader may be sure, Mr. Meeson did hold on pretty tight till, after rowing about fifty yards, the two men halted, and proceeded, not without some risk and trouble—for there was a considerable sea running—to hoist Mr. Meeson's large form over the gunwale of the boat.

Meanwhile, the horrors on board the doomed ship were redoubling, as she slowly settled to her watery grave. Forward, the steam fog-horn was going unceasingly, bellowing like a thousand furious bulls; while, now and again, a rocket still shot up through the misty morning air. Round the boats a hideous war was being waged. Augusta saw a great number of men jump into one of the largest life-boats, which was still hanging to the davits, having evidently got the better of those who were attempting to fill it with the women and children. The next second they lowered the after tackle, but, by some hitch or misunderstanding, not the foremost one; with the result that the stern of the boat fell while the bow remained fixed, and every soul in it, some forty or fifty people, was shot out into the water. Another boat was overturned by a sea as it settled on the water. Another one, full of women and children, got to the water all right, but remained fastened to the ship by the bow tackle. When, a couple of minutes afterwards, the Kangaroo went down, nobody had a knife at hand wherewith to cut the rope, and the boat was dragged down with her, and all its occupants drowned. The remaining boats, with the exception of the one in which Lady Holmhurst was, and which had been got away before the rush began, were never lowered at all, or sank as soon as lowered. It was impossible to lower them owing to the mad behaviour of the panic-stricken crowds, who fought like wild beasts for a place in them. A few gentlemen and sober-headed sailors could do nothing against a mob of frantic creatures, each bent on saving his own life, if it cost the lives of all else on board.

And thus it was exactly twenty minutes from the time that the Kangaroo sank the whaler (for, although these events have taken some time to describe, they did not take long to enact) that her own hour came, and, with the exception of some eight-and-twenty souls, all told, the hour also of every living creature who had taken passage in her.

CHAPTER VIII.
KERGUELEN LAND.

As soon as Mr. Meeson, saved from drowning by her intervention, lay gasping at the bottom of the boat, Augusta, overcome by a momentary faintness, let her head fall forward on to the bundle of blankets in which she had wrapped up the child she had rescued, and who, too terrified to speak or cry, stared about him with wide-opened and frightened eyes. When she lifted it, a few seconds later, a ray from the rising sun had pierced the mist, and striking full on the sinking ship, as, her stern well out of the water and her bow well under it, she rolled sullenly to and fro in the trough of the heavy sea, seemed to wrap her from hull to truck in wild and stormy light.

"She's going!—by George, she's going!" said the seaman Johnnie; and as he said it the mighty ship slowly reared herself up on end. Slowly—very slowly, amidst the hideous and despairing shrieks of the doomed wretches on board of her, she lifted her stern higher and higher, and plunged her bows deeper and deeper. They shrieked, they cried to Heaven for help; but Heaven heeded them not, for man's agony cannot avert man's doom. Now, for a space, she was standing almost upright upon the water, out of which about a hundred feet of her vast length towered like some monstrous ocean growth, whilst men fell from her in showers, like flies benumbed by frost, down into the churning foam beneath. Then suddenly, with a swift and awful rush, with a rending sound of breaking spars, a loud explosion of her boilers, and a smothered boom of bursting bulkheads, she plunged down into the measureless deeps, and was seen no more forever.

The water closed in over where she had been, boiling and foaming and sucking down all things in the wake of her last journey, while the steam and prisoned air came up in huge hissing jets and bubbles that exploded into spray on the surface.

The men groaned, the child stared stupefied, and Augusta cried out, "*Oh! oh*!" like one in pain.

"Row back!" she gasped, "row back and see if we cannot pick some of them up."

"No! no!" shouted Meeson; "they will sink the boat!"

"'Taint much use anyway," said Johnnie. "I doubt that precious few of them will come up again. They have gone too deep!"

However, they got the boat's head round again—slowly enough, Augusta thought—and as they did so they heard a feeble cry or two. But by the time that they had reached the spot where the Kangaroo went down, there was no living creature to be seen; nothing but the wash of the great waves, over which the mist once more closed thick and heavy as a pall. They shouted, and once they heard a faint answer, and rowed towards it; but when they got to the spot whence the sound seemed to proceed, they could see nothing except some wreckage. They were all dead, their agony was done, their cries no more ascended to the pitiless heavens; and wind, and sky, and sea were just as they had been.

"Oh, my God! my God!" wept Augusta, clinging to the thwarts of the tossing boat.

"One boat got away—where is it?" asked Mr. Meeson, who, a wet and wretched figure, was huddled up in the stern-sheets, as he rolled his wild eyes round striving to pierce the curtain of the mist.

"There's something," said Johnnie, pointing through a fog-dog in the mist, that seemed to grow denser rather than otherwise as the light increased, at a round, boat-like object that had suddenly appeared to the starboard of them.

They rowed up to it; it was a boat, but empty and floating bottom upwards. Closer examination showed that it was the cutter, which, when full of women and children, had been fastened to the vessel and dragged down with her as she sank. At a certain depth the pressure of the water had been too great and had torn the ring in the bow bodily out of her, so that she returned to the surface. But those in her did not return—at least, not yet. Once more, two or three days hence, they would arise from the watery depths and look upon the skies with eyes that could not see, and then vanish for ever.

Turning from this awful and most moving sight, they rowed slowly through quantities of floating wreckage—barrels, hencoops (in one of these they found two drowned fowls, which they secured), and many other articles, such as oars and wicker deck-chairs—and began to shout vigorously in the hope of attracting the attention of the survivors in the other boat, which they imagined could not be far off. Their efforts, however, proved fruitless, owing to the thickness of the fog; and in the considerable sea which was running it was impossible to see more than twenty yards or so. Also, what between the wind, and the wash and turmoil of the water, the sound of their voices did not travel far. The ocean is a large place, and a rowing-boat is easily lost sight of upon its furrowed surface; therefore it is not wonderful that, although the two boats were at the moment within half a mile of each other, they never met, and each took its separate course in the hope of escaping the fate of the vessel. The boat in which were Lady Holmhurst and some twenty other passengers, together with the second officer and a crew of six men, after seeing the Kangaroo sink and picking up one survivor, shaped a course for Kerguelen Land, believing that they, and they alone, remained to tell the tale of that awful shipwreck. And here it may be convenient to state that before nightfall they were picked up by a sealing-whaler, that sailed with them to Albany, on the coast of Australia. Thence an account of the disaster, which, as the reader will remember, created a deep impression, was telegraphed home, and thence, in due course, the widowed Lady Holmhurst and most of the other women who escaped were taken back to England.

To return to our heroine and Mr. Meeson.

The occupants of the little boat sat looking at each other with white scared faces, till at last the man called Johnnie, who, by-the-way, was not a tar of a very amiable cast of countenance, possibly owing to the fact that his nose was knocked almost flat against the side of his face, swore violently, and said "It was no good stopping there all the etceteraed day." Thereupon Bill, who was a more jovial-looking man, remarked "that he, Johnnie, was etceteraed well right, so they had better hoist the fore-sail."

At this point Augusta interposed, and told them that the captain, just as the vessel came into collision, had informed her that he was making Kerguelen Land, which was not more than sixty or seventy miles away. They had a compass in the boat, and they knew the course the Kangaroo was steering when she sank. Accordingly, without wasting further time, they got as much sail up as the little boat could carry in the stiff breeze, and ran nearly due east before the steady westerly wind. All day long they ran across the misty ocean, the little boat behaving splendidly, without sighting any living thing, till, at last, the night closed in again. There was, fortunately, a bag of biscuits in the boat, and a breaker of water; also there was, unfortunately, a breaker of rum, from which the two sailors, Bill and Johnnie, were already taking quite as much as was good for them. Consequently, though they were cold and wet with the spray, they had not to face the added horrors of starvation and thirst. At sundown, they shortened sail considerably, only leaving enough canvas up to keep the boat ahead of the sea.

Somehow the long night wore away. Augusta scarcely closed her eyes; but little Dick slept like a top upon her bosom, sheltered by her arms and the blanket from the cold and penetrating spray. In the bottom of the boat lay Mr. Meeson, to whom Augusta, pitying his condition—for he was shivering dreadfully—had given the other blanket, keeping nothing for herself except the woollen shawl.

At last, however, there came a faint glow in the east, and the daylight began to break over the stormy sea. Augusta turned her head and stared through the mist.

"What is that?" she said, in a voice trembling with excitement, to the sailor Bill, who was taking his turn at the tiller; and she pointed to a dark mass that loomed up almost over them.

The man looked, and then looked again; and then halloaed out joyfully, "Land—land ahead!"

Up struggled Mr. Meeson on to his knees—his legs were so stiff that he could not stand—and began to stare wildly about him.

"Thank God!" he cried. "Where is it? Is it New Zealand? If ever I get there, I'll stop there. I'll never get on a ship again!"

"New Zealand!" growled the sailor. "Are you a fool? It's Kerguelen Land, that's what it is—where it rains all day, and nobody lives—not even a nigger. It's like enough that you'll stop there, though; for I don't reckon that anybody will come to take you off in a hurry."

Mr. Meeson collapsed with a groan, and a few minutes afterwards the sun rose, while the mist grew less and less till at last it almost disappeared, revealing a grand panorama to the occupants of the boat. For before them was line upon line of jagged and lofty peaks, stretching as far as the eye could reach, gradually melting in the distance into the cold white gleam of snow. Bill slightly altered the boat's course to the southward, and, sailing round a point, she came into comparatively calm water. Then, due north of them, running into the land, they saw the mouth of a great fjord, bounded on each side by towering mountain banks, so steep as to be almost precipitous, around whose lofty sides thousands of sea fowl wheeled, awaking the echoes with their clamour. Right into this beautiful fjord they sailed, past a line of flat rocks on which sat huge fantastic monsters that the sailors said were sea-lions, along the line of beetling cliff, till they came to a spot where the shore, on which grew a rank, sodden-looking grass, shelved gently up from the water's edge to the frowning and precipitous background. And here, to their huge delight, they discovered two huts roughly built of old ship's timbers, placed within a score of yards of each other, and a distance of some fifty paces from the water's edge.

"Well, there's a house, anyway," said the flat-nosed Johnnie, "though it don't look as though it had paid rates and taxes lately."

"Let us land, and get out of this horrible boat," said Mr. Meeson, feebly: a proposition that Augusta seconded heartily enough. Accordingly, the sail was lowered, and, getting out the oars, the two sailors rowed the boat into a little, natural harbour that opened out of the main creek, and in ten minutes her occupants were once more stretching their legs upon dry land; that is, if any land in Kerguelen Island, that region of perpetual wet, could be said to be dry.

Their first care was to go up to the huts and examine them, with a result that could scarcely be called encouraging. The huts had been built some years—whether by the expedition which, in 1874, came thither to observe the transit of Venus, or by former parties of shipwrecked mariners, they never discovered—and were now in a state of ruin. Mosses and lichens grew plentifully upon the beams, and even on the floor; while great holes in the roof let in the wet, which lay in little slimy puddles beneath. Still, with all their drawbacks, they were decidedly better than the open beach; a very short experience of which, in that inclement climate, would certainly have killed them; and they thankfully decided to make the best of them. Accordingly, the smaller of the two huts was given up to Augusta and the boy Dick, while Mr. Meeson and the sailors took possession of the large one. Their next task was to move up their scanty belongings (the boat having first been carefully beached), and to clean out the huts and make them as habitable as possible by stretching the sails of the boat on the damp floors and covering up the holes in the roof as best they could with stones and bits of board from the bottom of the boat. The weather was, fortunately, dry, and as they all (with the exception of Mr. Meeson, who seemed to be quite prostrated) worked with a will, not excepting Master Dick—who toddled backwards and forwards after Augusta in high glee at finding himself on terra firma—and by midday everything that could be done was done. Then they made a fire of some drift-wood—for, fortunately, they had a few matches—and Augusta cooked the two fowls they had got out of the floating hen-coop as well as circumstances would allow—which, as a matter of fact, was not very well—and they had dinner, of which they all stood sadly in need.

After dinner they reckoned up their resources. Of water there was an ample supply, for not far from the huts a stream ran down into the fjord. For food they had the best part of a bag of biscuits weighing about a hundred pounds. Also there was the cask of rum, which the men had moved into their own hut. But that was not all, for there were plenty of shellfish about if they could find means to cook them, while the rocks around were covered with hundreds of penguins, including specimens of the great "King penguin," which only required to be knocked on the head. There was, therefore, little fear of their perishing of starvation, as sometimes happens to ship wrecked people. Indeed, immediately after dinner, the two sailors went out and returned with as many birds' eggs—mostly penguin—as they could carry in their hats. Scarcely had they got in, however, when the rain, which is the prevailing characteristic of these latitudes, set in, in the most pitiless fashion; and soon the great mountains with which they were surrounded, and those before them, were wrapped in dense veils of fleecy vapour. Hour after hour the rain fell without ceasing, penetrating through their miserable roof, and falling—drop, drip, drop—upon the sodden floor. Augusta sat by herself in the smaller hut, doing what she could to amuse little Dick by telling him stories. Nobody knows how hard she found it to have to invent stories when she was thus overwhelmed with misfortune; but it was the only way of keeping the poor child from crying, as the sense of cold and misery forced itself into his little heart. So she told him about Robinson Crusoe, and then she told him that they were playing at being Robinson Crusoe, to which the child very sensibly replied that he did not at all like the game, and wanted his mamma.

And meanwhile it grew darker and colder and damper hour by hour, till at last the light went out, and left her with nothing to keep her company but the moaning wind, the falling rain, and the wild cries of the sea-birds when something disturbed them from their rest. The child was asleep at last, wrapped up in a blanket and one of the smaller sails; and Augusta, feeling quite worn out with solitude and the pressure of heavy thoughts, began to think that the best thing she could do would be to try to follow his example, when suddenly there came a knock at the boards which served for a door to the shanty.

"Who is it?" she cried, with a start.

"Me—Mr. Meeson," answered a voice. "Can I come in?"

"Yes; if you like," said Augusta, sharply, though in her heart she was really glad to see him, or, rather, to hear him, for it was too dark to see anything. It is wonderful how, under the pressure of a great calamity, we forget our quarrels and our spites, and are ready to jump at the prospect of the human companionship of our deadliest enemy. And "the moral of that is," as the White Queen says, that as we are all night and day face to face with the last dread calamity—Death—we should throughout our lives behave as though we saw the present shadow of his hand. But that will never happen in the world while human nature is human nature—and when will it become anything else?

"Put up the door again," said Augusta, when, from a rather rawer rush of air than usual, she gathered that her visitor was within the hut.

Mr. Meeson obeyed, groaning audibly. "Those two brutes are getting drunk," he said, "swallowing down rum by the gallon. I have come because I could not stop with them any longer—and I am so ill, Miss Smithers, so ill! I believe that I am going to die. Sometimes I feel as though all the marrow in my bones were ice, and—and—at others just as though somebody were shoving a red-hot wire up them. Can't you do anything for me?"

"I don't see what is to be done," answered Augusta, gently, for the man's misery touched her in spite of her dislike for him. "You had better lie down and try to go to sleep."

"To sleep!" he moaned; "how can I sleep? My blanket is wringing wet and my clothes are damp," and he fairly broke down and began to groan and sob.

"Try and go to sleep," urged Augusta again.

He made no answer, but by degrees he grew quieter, overwhelmed, perhaps, by the solemn presence of the darkness. Augusta laid her head against the biscuit-bag, and at last sank into blissful oblivion; for to the young, sleep is a constant friend. Once or twice she woke, but only to drop off again; and when she finally opened her eyes it was quite light and the rain had ceased.

Her first care was for little Dick, who had slept soundly throughout the night and appeared to be none the worse. She took him outside the hut and washed his face and hands in the stream and then sat him down to a breakfast of biscuit. As she returned she met the two sailors, who, although they were now fairly sober, bore upon their faces the marks of a fearful debauch. Evidently they had been drinking heavily. She drew herself up and looked at them, and they slunk past her in silence.

Then she returned to the hut. Mr. Meeson was sitting up when she entered, and the bright light from the open door fell full upon his face. His appearance fairly shocked her. The heavy cheeks had fallen in, there were great purple rings round his hollow eyes, and his whole aspect was one of a man in the last stage of illness.

"I have had such a night" he said, "Oh, Heaven! such a night! I don't believe that I shall live through another."

"Nonsense!" said Augusta, "eat some biscuit and you will feel better."

He took a piece of the biscuit which she gave him, and attempted to swallow it, but could not.

"It is no use," he said; "I am a dying man. Sitting in those wet clothes in the boat has finished me."

And Augusta, looking at his face, could not but believe him.

CHAPTER IX.
AUGUSTA TO THE RESCUE.

After breakfast—that is, after Augusta had eaten some biscuit and a wing that remained from the chickens she had managed to cook upon the previous day—Bill and Johnnie, the two sailors, set to work, at her suggestion, to fix up a long fragment of drift-wood on a point of rock, and to bind it on to a flag that they happened to find in the locker of the boat. There was not much chance of its being seen by anybody in that mist-laden atmosphere, even if anybody came there to see it, of which there was still less chance; still they did it as a sort of duty. By the time this task was finished it was midday, and, for a wonder, there was little wind, and the sun shone out brightly. On returning to the huts Augusta got the blankets out to dry, and set the two sailors to roast some of the eggs they had found on the previous day. This they did willingly enough, for they were now quite sober, and very much ashamed of themselves. Then, after giving Dick some more biscuit and four roasted eggs, which he took to wonderfully, she went to Mr. Meeson, who was lying groaning in the hut, and persuaded him to come and sit out in the warmth.

By this time the wretched man's condition was pitiable, for, though his strength was still whole in him, he was persuaded that he was going to die, and could touch nothing but some rum-and-water.

"Miss Smithers," he said, as he sat shivering upon the rocks, "I am going to die in this horrible place, and I am not fit to die! To think of me," he went on with a sudden burst of his old fire, "to think of me dying like a starved dog in the cold, when I have two millions of money waiting to be spent there in England! And I would give them all—yes, every farthing of them—to find myself safe at home again! By Jove! I would change places with any poor devil of a writer in the Hutches! Yes, I would turn author on twenty pounds a month!—that will give you some idea of my condition, Miss Smithers! To think that I should ever live to say that I would care to be a beggarly author, who could not make a thousand a year if he wrote till his fingers fell off!—oh! oh!" and he fairly sobbed at the horror and degradation of the thought.

Augusta looked at the poor wretch and then bethought her of the proud creature she had known, raging terribly through the obsequious ranks of clerks, and carrying desolation to the Hutches and the many-headed editorial department. She looked, and was filled with reflections on the mutability of human affairs.

Alas! how changed that Meeson!

"Yes," he went on, recovering himself a little, "I am going to die in this horrible place, and all my money will not even give me a decent funeral. Addison and Roscoe will get it—confound them!—as though they had not got enough already. It makes me mad when I think of those Addison girls spending my money, or bribing Peers to marry them with it, or something of that sort. I disinherited my own nephew, Eustace, and kicked him out to sink or swim; and now I can't undo it, and I would give anything to alter it! We quarrelled about you, Miss Smithers, because I would not give you any more money for that book of yours. I wish I had given it to you—anything you wanted. I didn't treat you well; but, Miss Smithers, a bargain is a bargain. It would never have done to give way, on principle. You must understand that, Miss Smithers. Don't revenge yourself on me about it, now that I am helpless, because, you see, it was a matter of principle."

"I am not in the habit of revenging myself, Mr. Meeson," answered Augusta, with dignity; "but I think that you have done a very wicked thing to disinherit your nephew in that fashion, and I don't wonder that you feel uncomfortable about it."

The expression of this vigorous opinion served to disturb Mr. Meeson's conscience all the more, and he burst out into laments and regrets.

"Well," said Augusta at last, "if you don't like your will you had better alter it. There are enough of us here to witness a will, and, if anything happens to you, it will override the other—will it not?"

This was a new idea, and the dying man jumped at it.

"Of course, of course," he said; "I never thought of that before. I will do it at once, and cut Addison and Roscoe out altogether. Eustace shall have every farthing. I never thought of that before. Come, give me your hand; I'll get up and see about it."

"Stop a minute," said Augusta. "How are you going to write a will without pen or pencil, or paper or ink?"

Mr. Meeson sank back with a groan. This difficulty had not occurred to him.

"Are you sure nobody has got a pencil and a bit of paper?" he asked. "It would do, so long as the writing remained legible."

"I don't think so," said Augusta, "but I will inquire." Accordingly she went and asked Bill and Johnnie: but neither of them had a pencil or a single scrap of paper, and she returned sadly to communicate the news.

"I have got it, I have got it," said Mr. Meeson, as she approached the spot where he lay upon the rock. "If there is no paper or pen, we must write it in blood upon some linen. We can make a pen from the feathers of a bird. I read somewhere in a book of somebody who did that. It will do as well as anything else."

Here was an idea, indeed, and one that Augusta jumped at. But in another moment her enthusiasm received a check. Where was there any linen to write on?

"Yes," she said, "if you can find some linen. You have got on a flannel shirt, so have the two sailors, and little Dick is dressed in flannel, too."

It was a fact. As it happened, not one of the party had a scrap of linen on them, or anything that would answer the purpose. Indeed, they had only one pocket-handkerchief between them, and it was a red rag full of holes. Augusta had had one, but it had blown overboard when they were in the boat. What would they not have given for that pocket-handkerchief now!

"Yes," said Mr. Meeson, "it seems we have none. I haven't even get a bank-note, or I might have written in blood upon that; though I have got a hundred sovereigns in gold—I grabbed them up before I bolted from the cabin. But I say—excuse me, Miss Smithers, but—um—ah—oh! hang modesty—haven't you got some linen on, somewhere or other, that you could spare a bit of? You shan't lose by giving it to me. There, I promise that I will tear up the agreement if ever I get out of this—which I shan't—which I shan't—and I will write on the linen that it is to be torn up. Yes, and that you are to have five thousand pounds legacy too, Miss Smithers. Surely you can spare me a little bit—just off the skirt, or somewhere, you know, Miss Smithers? It never will be missed, and it is so *very* important."

Augusta blushed, and no wonder. "I am sorry to say I have nothing of the sort about me, Mr. Meeson—nothing except flannel," she said. "I got up in the middle of the night before the collision, and there was no light in the cabin, and I put on whatever came first, meaning to come back and dress afterwards when it got light."

"Stays!" said Mr. Meeson, desperately. "Forgive me for mentioning them, but surely you put on your stays? One could write on them, you know."

"I am very sorry, Mr. Meeson," she answered, "but I did not put any on."

"Not a cuff or a collar?" he said, catching at a last straw of hope.

Augusta shook her head sadly.

"Then there is an end of it!" groaned Mr. Meeson. "Eustace must lose the money. Poor lad! poor lad! I have behaved very badly to him."

Augusta stood still, racking her brain for some expedient, for she was determined that Eustace Meeson should not lose the chance of that colossal fortune if she could help it. It was but a poor chance at the best, for Mr.

Meeson might not be dying, after all. And if he did die, it was probable that his fate would be their fate also, and no record would remain of them or of Mr. Meeson's testamentary wishes. As things looked at present, there was every prospect of their all perishing miserably on that desolate shore.

Just then the sailor Bill, who had been up to the flagstaff on the rock on the chance of catching sight of some passing vessel, came walking past. His flannel shirt-sleeves were rolled up to the elbows of his brawny arms, and as he stopped to speak to Augusta she noticed something that made her start, and gave her an idea.

"There ain't nothing to be seen," said the man, roughly; "and it is my belief that there won't be neither. Here we are, and here we stops till we dies and rots."

"Ah, I hope not," said Augusta. "By-the-way, Mr. Bill, will you let me look at the tattoo on your arm?"

"Certainly, Miss," said Bill, with alacrity, holding his great arm within an inch of her nose. It was covered with various tattoos: flags, ships, and what not, in the middle of which, written in small letters along the side of the forearm, was the sailor's name—Bill Jones.

"Who did it, Mr. Bill?" asked Augusta.

"Who did it? Why I did it myself. A chap made me a bet that I could not tattoo my own name on my own arm, so I showed him; and a poor sort of hand I should have been at tattooing if I could not."

Augusta said no more till Bill had gone on, then she spoke.

"Now, Mr. Meeson, do you see how you can make your will?" she said quietly.

"See? No." he answered, "I don't."

"Well, I do: you can tattoo it—or, rather get the sailor to tattoo it. It need not be very long."

"Tattoo it! What on, and what with?" he asked, astonished.

"You can have it tattooed on the back of the other sailor, Johnnie, if he will allow you; and as for material, you have some revolver cartridges; if the gunpowder is mixed with water, it would do, I should think."

"'Pon my word," said Mr. Meeson, "you are a wonderful woman! Whoever would have thought of such a thing except a woman? Go and ask the man Johnnie, there's a good girl, if he would mind my will being tattooed upon his back."

"Well," said Augusta; "it's a queer sort of message; but I'll try." Accordingly, taking little Dick by the hand, she went across to where the two sailors were sitting outside their hut, and putting on her sweetest smile, first of all asked Mr. Bill if he would mind doing a little tattooing for her. To this Mr. Bill, finding time hang heavy upon his hands, and wishing to be kept out of the temptation of the rum-cask, graciously assented, saying that he had seen some sharp fish-bones lying about which would be the very thing, though he shook his head at the idea of using gunpowder as the medium. He said it would not do at all well, and then, as though suddenly seized by an inspiration, started off down to the shore.

Then Augusta, as gently and nicely as she could, approached the question with Johnnie, who was sitting with his back against the hut, his battered countenance wearing a peculiarly ill-favored expression, probably owing to the fact that he was suffering from severe pain in his head, as a result of the debauch of the previous night.

Slowly and with great difficulty, for his understanding was none of the clearest, she explained to him what was required; and that it was suggested that he should provide the necessary *corpus vile* upon which it was proposed that the experiment should be made. When at last he understood what it was asked that he should do, Johnnie's countenance was a sight to see, and his language was more striking than correct. The upshot of it was, however, that he would see Mr. Meeson collectively, and Mr. Meeson's various members separately, especially his eyes, somewhere first.

Augusta retreated till his wrath had spent itself, and then once more returned to the charge.

She was sure, she said, that Mr. Johnnie would not mind witnessing the document, if anybody else could be found to submit to the pain of the tattooing. All that would be necessary would be for him to touch the hand of the operator while his (Johnnie's) name was tattooed as witness to the will. "Well," he said, "I don't know how as I mind doing that, since it's you as asked me, Miss, and not the d——d old hulks of a Meeson. I would not lift a finger to save him from 'ell Miss, and that's a fact!"

"Then that is a promise, Mr. Johnnie?" said Augusta, sweetly ignoring the garnishing with which the promise was adorned; and on Mr. Johnnie stating that he looked at it in that light, she returned to Mr. Meeson. On her way she met Bill, carrying in his hands a loathsome-looking fish, with long feelers and a head like a parrot, in short, a cuttle-fish.

"Now, here's luck, Miss," said Bill, exultingly; "I saw this gentleman lying down on the beach there this morning. He's a cuttle, that's what he is; and

I'll have his ink-bag out of him in a brace of shakes; just the ticket for tattooing, Miss, as good as the best Indian-ink—gunpowder is a fool to it."

By this time they had reached Mr. Meeson, and here the whole matter, including Johnnie's obstinate refusal to be tattooed was explained to Bill.

"Well," said Augusta at length, "it seems that's the only thing to be done; but the question is, how to do it? I can only suggest, Mr. Meeson, that the will should be tattooed on you."

"Oh!" said Mr. Meeson, feebly, "on me! Me tattooed like a savage—tattooed with my own will!"

"It wouldn't be much use, either, governor, begging your pardon," said Bill, "that is, if you are agoing to croak, as you say; 'cause where would the will be then? We might skin you with a sharp stone, perhaps, after you've done the trick, you know," he added reflectively. "But then we have no salt, so I doubt if you'd keep; and if we set your hide in the sun, I reckon the writing would shrivel up so that all the courts of law in London could not make head or tail of it."

Mr. Meeson groaned loudly, as well he might. These frank remarks would have been trying to any man; much more were they so to this opulent merchant prince, who had always set the highest value on what Bill rudely called his "hide."

"There's the infant," went on Bill, meditatively. "He's young and white, and I fancy his top-crust would work wonderful easy; but you'd have to hold him, for I expect that he'd yell proper."

"Yes," said Mr. Meeson; "let the will be tattooed upon the child. He'd be some use that way."

"Yes," said Bill; "and there'd allus be something left to remind me of a very queer time, provided he lives to get out of it, which is doubtful. Cuttle-ink won't rub out, I'll warrant."

"I won't have Dick touched," said Augusta, indignantly. "It would frighten the child into fits; and, besides, nobody has a right to mark him for life in that way."

"Well, then, there's about an end of the question," said Bill; "and this gentleman's money must go wherever it is he don't want it to."

"No," said Augusta, with a sudden flush, "there is not. Mr. Eustace Meeson was once very kind to me, and rather than he should lose the chance of getting what he ought to have, I—I will be tattooed."

"Well, bust me!" said Bill, with enthusiasm, "bust me! if you ain't a good-plucked one for a female woman; and if I was that there young man I should make bold to tell you so."

"Yes," said Mr. Meeson, "that is an excellent idea. You are young and strong, and as there is lots of food here, I dare say that you will take a long time to die. You might even live for some months. Let us begin at once. I feel dreadfully weak. I don't think that I can live through the night, and if I know that I have done all I can to make sure that Eustace gets his own, perhaps dying will be a little easier!"

CHAPTER X.
THE LAST OF MR. MEESON.

Augusta turned from the old man with a gesture of impatience not unmixed with disgust. His selfishness was of an order that revolted her.

"I suppose," she said sharply to Bill, "that I must have this will tattooed upon my shoulders."

"Yes, Miss; that's it," said Bill. "You see, Miss, one wants space for a doccymint. If it were a ship or a flag, now, or a fancy pictur of your young man, I might manage it on your arm, but there must be breadth for a legal doccymint, more especially as I should like to make a good job of it while I is about it. I don't want none of them laryers a-turning up their noses at Bill Jones' tattooing."

"Very well," said Augusta, with an inward sinking of the heart; "I will go and get ready."

Accordingly she adjourned into the hut and removed the body of her dress and turned down the flannel garment underneath it in such a fashion as to leave as much of her neck bare as is to be seen when a lady has on a moderately low dress. Then she came out again, dressed, or rather undressed, for the sacrifice. Meanwhile, Bill had drawn out the ink-bag of the cuttle, had prepared a little round fragment of wood which he sharpened like a pencil by rubbing it against a stone, and had put a keen edge on to a long white fishbone that he had selected.

"Now, Mr. Bill, I am ready," said Augusta, seating herself resolutely upon a flat stone and setting her teeth.

"My word, Miss; but you have a fine pair of shoulders!" said the sailor, contemplating the white expanse with the eye of an artist. "I never had such a bit of material to work on afore. Hang me if it ain't almost a pity to mark 'em! Not but what high-class tattooing is an ornimint to anybody, from a Princess down; and in that you are fortunit, Miss, for I larnt tattooing from them as *can* tattoo, I did."

Augusta bit her lip, and the tears came into her eyes. She was only a woman, and had a woman's little weakness; and, though she had never appeared in a low dress in her life, she knew that her neck was one of her greatest beauties, and was proud of it. It was hard to think that she would be marked all her life with this ridiculous will—that is, if she escaped—and, what was more, for the benefit of a young man who had no claim upon her at all.

That was what she said to herself; but as she said it, something in her told her that it was not true. Something told her that this young Mr. Eustace

Meeson *had* a claim upon her—the highest claim that a man could have upon a woman, for the truth must out—she loved him. It seemed to have come home to her quite clearly here in this dreadful desolate place, here in the very shadow of an awful death, that she did love him, truly and deeply. And that being so, she would not have been what she was—a gentle-natured, devoted woman—had she not at heart rejoiced at this opportunity of self-sacrifice, even though that self-sacrifice was of the hardest sort, seeing that it involved what all women hate—the endurance of a ridiculous position. For love can do all things: it can even make its votaries brave ridicule.

"Go on," she said sharply, "and let us get it over as soon as possible."

"Very well, Miss. What is it to be, old gentleman? Cut it short, you know."

"'*I leave all my property to Eustace H. Meeson*,' that's as short as I can get it; and, if properly witnessed, I think that it will cover everything," said Mr. Meeson, with a feeble air of triumph. "Anyhow, I never heard of a will that is to carry about two millions being got into nine words before."

Bill poised his fishbone, and, next second, Augusta gave a start and a little shriek, for the operation had begun.

"Never mind, Miss," said Bill, consolingly; "you'll soon get used to it."

After that Augusta set her teeth and endured in silence, though it really hurt her very much, for Bill was more careful of the artistic effect and the permanence of the work than of the feelings of the subject. *Fiat experimentum in corpore vili*, he would have said had he been conversant with the Classics, without much consideration for the *corpus vile*. So he pricked and dug away with his fishbone, which he dipped continually in the cuttle-ink, and with the sharp piece of wood, till Augusta began to feel perfectly faint.

For three hours the work continued, and at the end of that time the body of the will was finished—for Bill was a rapid worker—being written in medium-sized letters right across her shoulders. But the signatures yet remained to be affixed.

Bill asked her if she would like to let them stand over till the morrow?—but this, although she felt ill with the pain she declined to do. She was marked now, marked with the ineffaceable mark of Bill, so she might as well be marked to some purpose. If she put off the signing of the document till the morrow, it might be too late, Mr. Meeson might be dead, Johnnie might have changed his mind, or a hundred things. So she told them to go on and finish it as quickly as possible, for there was only about two hours more daylight.

Fortunately Mr. Meeson was more or less acquainted with the formalities that are necessary in the execution of a will, namely: that the testator and the two witnesses should all sign in the presence of each other. He also knew that it was sufficient, if, in cases of illness, some third person held the pen between the testator's fingers and assisted him to write his name, or even if someone signed for the testator in his presence and by his direction; and, arguing from this knowledge, he came to the conclusion—afterwards justified in the great case of Meeson *v.* Addison and Another—that it would be sufficient if he inflicted the first prick of his signature, and then kept his hand upon Bill's while the rest was done. This accordingly, he did, clumsily running the point of the sharp bone so deep into the unfortunate Augusta that she fairly shrieked aloud, and then keeping his hand upon the sailor's arm while he worked in the rest of the signature, "*J. Meeson.*" When it was done, the turn of Johnnie came. Johnnie had at length aroused himself to some interest in what was going on, and had stood by watching all the time, since Mr. Meeson having laid his finger upon Augusta's shoulder, had solemnly declared the writing thereon to be his last will and testament. As he (Johnnie) could not tattoo, the same process was gone through with reference to his signature, as in the case of Mr. Meeson. Then Bill Jones signed his own name, as the second witness to the will; and just as the light went out of the sky the document was finally executed—the date of the execution being alone omitted. Augusta got up off the flat stone where she had been seated during this torture for something like five hours, and staggering into the hut, threw herself down upon the sail, and went off into a dead faint. It was indeed only by a very strong exercise of the will that she had kept herself from fainting long before.

The next thing she was conscious of was a dreadful smarting in her back, and on opening her eyes found that it was quite dark in the hut. So weary was she, however, that after stretching out her hand to assure herself that Dick was safe by her side, she shut her eyes again and went fast asleep. When she woke, the daylight was creeping into the damp and squalid hut, revealing the heavy form of Mr. Meeson tossing to and fro in a troubled slumber on the further side. She got up, feeling dreadfully sore about the back; and, awaking the child, took him out to the stream of water and washed him and herself as well as she could. It was very cold outside; so cold that the child cried, and the rain clouds were coming up fast, so she hurried back to the hut, and, together with Dick, made her breakfast off some biscuit and some roast penguin's eggs, which were not at all bad eating. She was indeed, quite weak with hunger, having swallowed no food for many hours, and felt proportionately better after it.

Then she turned to examine the condition of Mr. Meeson. The will had been executed none too soon, for it was evident to her that he was in a very bad way indeed. His face was sunken and hectic with fever, his teeth were chattering, and his talk, though he was now awake, was quite incoherent. She tried to get him to take some food; but he would swallow nothing but water.

Having done all that she could for him, she went out to see the sailors, and met them coming down from the flagstaff. They had evidently been, though not to any great extent, at the rum cask again, for Bill looked sheepish and shaky, while the ill-favored Johnnie was more sulky than ever. She gazed at them reproachfully, and then asked them to collect some more penguin's eggs, which Johnnie refused point-blank to do, saying that he wasn't going to collect eggs for landlubbers to eat; she might collect eggs for herself. Bill, however, started on the errand, and in about an hour's time returned, just as the rain set in in good earnest, bearing six or seven dozen fresh eggs tied up in his coat.

Augusta, with the child by her, sat in the miserable hut attending to Mr. Meeson; while outside the pitiless rain poured down in a steady unceasing sheet of water that came through the wretched roof in streams. She did her best to keep the dying man dry, but it proved to be almost an impossibility; for even when she succeeded in preventing the wet from falling on him from above, it got underneath him from the reeking floor, while the heavy damp of the air gathered on his garments till they were quite sodden.

As the hours went on his consciousness came back to him, and with it his terror for the end and his remorse for his past life, for alas! the millions he had amassed could not avail him now.

"I am going to die!" he groaned. "I am going to die, and I've been a bad man: I've been the head of a publishing company all my life!"

Augusta gently pointed out to him that publishing was a very respectable business when fairly and properly carried on, and not one that ought to weigh heavy upon a man at the last like the record of a career of successful usury or burgling.

He shook his heavy head. "Yes, yes," he groaned; "but Meeson's is a company and you are talking of private firms. They are straight, most of them; far too straight, I used always to say. But you don't know Meeson's—you don't know the customs of the trade at Meeson's."

Augusta reflected that she knew a good deal more about Meeson's than she liked.

"Listen," he said, with desperate energy, sitting up upon the sail, "and I will tell you—I must tell you."

Asterisks, so dear to the heart of the lady novelist, will best represent the confession that followed; words are not equal to the task.

Augusta listened with rising hair, and realised how very trying must be the life of a private confessor.

"Oh, please stop!" she said faintly, at last. "I can't bear it—I can't, indeed."

"Ah!" he said, as he sunk back exhausted. "I thought that when you understood the customs at Meeson's you would feel for me in my present position. Think, girl, think what I must suffer, with such a past, standing face to face with an unknown future!"

Then came a silence.

"Take him away! Take him away!" suddenly shouted out Mr. Meeson, staring around him with frightened eyes.

"Who?" asked Augusta; "who?"

"Him—the tall, thin man, with the big book! I know him; he used to be Number 25—he died years ago. He was a very clever doctor; but one of his patients brought a false charge against him and ruined him, so he had to take to writing, poor devil! We made him edit a medical encyclopaedia—twelve volumes for £300, to be paid on completion; and he went mad and died at the eleventh volume. So, of course, we did not pay his widow anything. And now he's come for me—I know he has. Listen! he's talking! Don't you hear him? Oh, Heavens! He says that I am going to be an author, and he is going to publish for me for a thousand years—going to publish on the quarter-profit system, with an annual account, the usual trade deductions, and no vouchers. Oh! oh! Look!—they are all coming!—they are pouring out of the Hutches! they are going to murder me!—keep them off! keep them off!" and he howled and beat the air with his hands.

Augusta, utterly overcome by this awful sight, knelt down by his side and tried to quiet him, but in vain. He continued beating his hands in the air, trying to keep off the ghostly train, till, at last, with one awful howl, he fell back dead.

And that was the end of Meeson. And the works that he published, and the money that he made, and the house that he built, and the evil that he did—are they not written in the Book of the Commercial Kings?

"Well," said Augusta faintly to herself when she had got her breath back a little, "I am glad that it is over; anyway, I do hope that I may never be called on to nurse the head of another publishing company."

"Auntie! auntie!" gasped Dick, "why do the gentleman shout so?"

Then, taking the frightened child by the hand, Augusta made her way through the rain to the other hut, in order to tell the two sailors what had come to pass. It had no door, and she paused on the threshold to prospect.

The faint foggy light was so dim that at first she could see nothing. Presently, however, her eyes got accustomed to it, and she made out Bill and Johnnie sitting opposite to each other on the ground. Between them was the breaker of rum. Bill had a large shell in his hand, which he had just filled from the cask; for Augusta saw him in the act of replacing the spigot.

"My go!—curse you, my go!" said Johnnie, as Bill lifted the shell of spirits to his lips. "You've had seven goes and I've only had six!"

"You be blowed!" said Bill, swallowing the liquor in a couple of great gulps. "Ah! that's better! Now I'll fill for you, mate: fair does, I says, fair does and no favour," and he filled accordingly.

"Mr. Meeson is dead," said Augusta, screwing up her courage to interrupt this orgie.

The two men stared at her in drunken surprise, which Johnnie broke.

"Now is he, Miss?" he said, with a hiccough: "is he? Well, a good job too, says I; a useless old landlubber he was. I doubt he's off to a warmer place than this 'ere Kerguelen Land, and I drinks his health, which, by-the-way, I never had the occasion to do before. Here's to the health of the departed," and he swallowed the shellfull of rum at a draught.

"Your sentiment I echoes," said Bill. "Johnnie, the shell; give us the shell to drink the 'ealth of the dear departed."

Then Augusta returned to her hut with a heavy heart. She covered up the dead body as best she could, telling little Dick that Mr. Meeson was gone by-by, and then sat down in that chill and awful company. It was very depressing; but she comforted herself somewhat with the reflection that, on the whole, Mr. Meeson dead was not so bad as Mr. Meeson in the animated flesh.

Presently the night set in once more, and, worn out with all that she had gone through, Augusta said her prayers and went to sleep with little Dick locked fast in her arms.

Some hours afterwards she was awakened by loud and uproarious shouts, made up of snatches of drunken songs and that peculiar class of English that hovers ever round the lips of the British Tar. Evidently Bill and Johnnie were raging drunk, and in this condition were taking the midnight air.

The shouting and swearing went reeling away towards the water's edge, and then, all of a sudden, they culminated in a fearful yell—after which came silence.

What could it mean? wondered Augusta and whilst she was still wondering dropped off to sleep again.

CHAPTER XI.
RESCUED.

Augusta woke up just as the dawn was stealing across the sodden sky. It was the smarting of her shoulders that woke her. She rose, leaving Dick yet asleep, and, remembering the turmoil of the night, hurried to the other hut. It was empty.

She turned and looked about her. About fifteen paces from where she was lay the shell that the two drunkards had used as a cup. Going forward, she picked it up. It still smelt disgustingly of spirits. Evidently the two men had dropped it in the course of their midnight walk, or rather roll. Where had they gone to?

Straight in front of her a rocky promontory ran out fifty paces or more into the waters of the fjord-like bay. She walked along it aimlessly till presently she perceived one of the sailor's hats lying on the ground, or, rather, floating in a pool of water. Clearly they had gone this way. On she went to the point of the little headland, sheer over the water. There was nothing to be seen, not a single vestige of Bill and Johnnie. Aimlessly enough she leant forward and stared over the rocky wall, and down into the clear water, and then started back with a little cry.

No wonder that she started, for there on the sand, beneath a fathom and a half of quiet water, lay the bodies of the two ill-fated men. They were locked in each other's arms, and lay as though they were asleep upon that ocean bed. How they came to their end she never knew. Perhaps they quarrelled in their drunken anger and fell over the little cliff; or perhaps they stumbled and fell not knowing whither they were going. Who can say? At any rate, there they were, and there they remained, till the outgoing tide floated them off to join the great army of their companions who had gone down with the Kangaroo. And so Augusta was left alone.

With a heavy heart she returned to the hut, pressed down by the weight of solitude, and the sense that in the midst of so much death she could not hope to escape. There was no human creature left alive in that vast lonely land, except the child and herself, and so far as she could see their fate would soon be as the fate of the others. When she got back to the hut, Dick was awake and was crying for her.

The still, stiff form of Mr. Meeson, stretched out beneath the sail, frightened the little lad, he did not know why. Augusta took him into her arms and kissed him passionately. She loved the child for his own sake; and, besides, he, and he alone, stood between her and utter solitude. Then she took him across to the other hut, which had been vacated by the sailors, for it was impossible to stay in the one with the body, which was too heavy for her to move. In the centre of the sailors' hut stood the cask of rum which had been the cause of their destruction. It was nearly empty now—so light, indeed, that she had no difficulty in rolling it to one side. She cleaned out the place as well as she could, and returning to where Mr. Meeson's body lay, fetched the bag of biscuits and the roasted eggs, after which they had their breakfast.

Fortunately there was but little rain that morning, so Augusta took Dick out to look for eggs, not because they wanted any more, but in order to employ themselves. Together they climbed up on to a rocky headland, where the flag was flying, and looked out across the troubled ocean. There was nothing in sight so far as the eye could see—nothing but the white wave-horses across which the black cormorants steered their swift, unerring flight. She looked and looked till her heart sank within her.

"Will Mummy soon come in a boat to take Dick away?" asked the child at her side, and then she burst into tears.

When she had recovered herself they set to collecting eggs, an occupation which, notwithstanding the screams and threatened attacks of the birds, delighted Dick greatly. Soon they had as many as she could carry; so they went back to the hut and lit a fire of drift-wood, and roasted some eggs in the hot ashes; she had no pot to boil them in. Thus, one way and another the day wore away, and at last the darkness began to fall over the rugged peaks behind and the wild wilderness of sea before. She put Dick to bed and he went off to sleep. Indeed, it was wonderful to see how well the child bore the hardships through which they were passing. He never had an ache or a pain, or even a cold in the head.

After Dick was asleep Augusta sat, or rather lay, in the dark listening to the moaning of the wind as it beat upon the shanty and passed away in gusts among the cliffs and mountains beyond. The loneliness was something awful, and together with the thought of what the end of it would probably be, quite broke her spirit down. She knew that the chances of her escape were small indeed. Ships did not often come to this dreadful and uninhabited coast, and if one should happen to put in there, it was exceedingly probable that it would touch at some other point and never see her or her flag. And then in time the end would come. The supply of eggs would fail, and she would be driven to supporting life upon such birds as she could catch, till at last the child sickened and died, and she followed it to that dim land that lies beyond Kerguelen and the world. She prayed that the child might die first. It was awful to think that perhaps it might be the other way about: she might die first, and the child might be left to starve beside her. The morrow would be Christmas Day. Last Christmas Day she had spent with her dead sister at Birmingham. She remembered that they went to church in the morning, and after dinner she had finished correcting the last revises of "Jemima's Vow." Well, it seemed likely that long before another Christmas came she would have gone to join little Jeannie. And then, being a good and religious girl, Augusta rose to her knees and prayed to Heaven with all her heart and soul to rescue them from their terrible position, or, if she was doomed to perish, at least to save the child.

And so the long cold night wore away in thought and vigil, till at last, some two hours before the dawn, she got to sleep. When she opened her eyes again it was broad daylight, and little Dick, who had been awake some time beside her, was sitting up playing with the shell which Bill and Johnnie had used to drink rum out of. She rose and put the child's things a little to rights, and then, as it was not raining, told him to run outside while she went through the form of dressing by taking off such garments as she had, shaking them, and putting them on again. She was slowly going through this process, and wondering how long it would be before her shoulders ceased to smart from the effects of the tattooing, when Dick came running in without going through the formality of knocking.

"Oh, Auntie! Auntie!" he sang out in high glee, "here's a big ship coming sailing along. Is it Mummie and Daddie coming to fetch Dick?"

Augusta sank back faint with the sudden revulsion of feeling. If there was a ship, they were saved—snatched from the very jaws of death. But perhaps it was the child's fancy. She threw on the body of her dress; and, her long yellow hair—which she had in default of better means been trying to comb out with a bit of wood—streaming behind her, she took the child by the hand, and flew as fast as she could go down the little rocky promontory off which Bill and Johnnie had met their end. Before she got half-way down it, she saw that the child's tale was true—for there, sailing right up the fjord from the open sea, was a large vessel. She was not two hundred yards from where she stood, and her canvas was being rapidly furled preparatory to the anchor being dropped.

Thanking Providence for the sight as she never thanked anything before, Augusta sped on till she got to the extreme point of the promontory, and stood there waving Dick's little cap towards the vessel, which moved slowly and majestically on, till presently, across the clear water, came the splash of the anchor, followed by the sound of the fierce rattle of the chain through the hawse-pipes. Then there came another sound—the glad sound of human voices cheering. She had been seen.

Five minutes passed, and then she saw a boat lowered and manned. The oars were got out, and presently it was backing water within ten paces of her.

"Go round there," she called, pointing to the little bay, "and I will meet you."

By the time that she had got to the spot the boat was already beached, and a tall, thin, kindly-faced man was addressing her in an unmistakable Yankee accent, "Cast away, Miss?" he said interrogatively.

"Yes," gasped Augusta; "we are the survivors of the Kangaroo, which sank in a collision with a whaler about a week ago."

"Ah!" said the captain, "with a whaler? Then I guess that's where my consort has gone to. She's been missing about a week, and I put in here to see if I could get upon her tracks—also to fill up with water. Well, she was well insured, anyway, and when last we spoke her, she had made a very poor catch. But perhaps, Miss, you will, at your convenience, favour me with a few particulars?"

Accordingly, Augusta sketched the history of their terrible adventure in as few words as possible; and the tale was one that made even the phlegmatic Yankee captain stare. Then she took him, followed by the crew, to the hut where Meeson lay dead, and to the other hut, where she and Dick had slept upon the previous night.

"Wall, Miss," said the captain, whose name was Thomas, "I guess that you and the youngster will be almost ready to vacate these apartments; so, if you please, I will send you off to the ship, the Harpoon—that's her name—of Norfolk, in the United States. You will find her well flavoured with oil, for we are about full to the hatches; but, perhaps, under the circumstances, you will not mind that. Anyway, my Missus, who is aboard—having come the cruise for her health—and who is an Englishwoman like you, will do all she can to make you comfortable. And I tell you what it is, Miss; if I was in any way pious, I should just thank the Almighty that I happened to see that there bit of a flag with my spyglass as I was sailing along the coast at sun-up this morning, for I had no intention of putting in at this creek, but at one twenty miles along. And now, Miss, if you'll go aboard, some of us will stop and just tuck up the dead gentleman as well as we can."

Augusta thanked him from her heart, and, going into the hut, got her hat and the roll of sovereigns which had been Mr. Meeson's, but which he had told her to take, leaving the blankets to be brought by the men.

Then two of the sailors got into the little boat belonging to the Kangaroo, in which Augusta had escaped, and rowed her and Dick away from that hateful shore to where the whaler—a fore-and-aft-schooner—was lying at anchor. As they drew near, she saw the rest of the crew of the Harpoon, among whom was a woman, watching their advent from the deck, who, when she got her foot upon the companion ladder, one and all set up a hearty cheer. In another moment she was on deck—which, notwithstanding its abominable smell of oil, seemed to her the fairest and most delightful place that her eyes had ever rested on—and being almost hugged by Mrs. Thomas, a pleasant-looking woman of about thirty, the daughter of a Suffolk farmer who had emigrated to the States. And then, of course, she had to tell her story all over again; after which she was led off to the cabin occupied by the captain and his wife (and which thenceforth was occupied by Augusta, Mrs. Thomas, and little Dick), the captain shaking down where he could. And here, for the first time for nearly a week, she was able to wash and dress herself properly. And oh, the luxury of it! Nobody knows what the delights of clean linen really mean till he or she has had to dispense with it under circumstances of privation; nor have they the slightest idea of what a difference to one's well-being and comfort is made by the possession or non-possession of an article so common as a comb. Whilst Augusta was still combing out her hair with sighs of delight, Mrs. Thomas knocked at the door and was admitted.

"My! Miss; what beautiful hair you have, now that it is combed out!" she said in admiration; "why, whatever is that upon your shoulders?"

Then Augusta had to tell the tale of the tattooing, which by the way, it struck her, it was wise to do, seeing that she thus secured a witness to the fact, that she was already tattooed on leaving Kerguelen Land, and that the operation had been of such recent infliction that the flesh was still inflamed with it. This was the more necessary as the tattooing was undated.

Mrs. Thomas listened to the story with her mouth open, lost between admiration of Augusta's courage, and regret that her shoulders should have been ruined in that fashion.

"Well, the least that he" (alluding to Eustace) "can do is to marry you after you have spoilt yourself in that fashion for his benefit," said the practical Mrs. Thomas.

"Nonsense! Mrs. Thomas," said Augusta, blushing till the tattoo marks on her shoulders looked like blue lines in a sea of crimson, and stamping her foot with such energy that her hostess jumped.

There was no reason why she should give an innocent remark such a warm reception; but then, as the reader will no doubt have observed, the reluctance that some young women show to talking of the possibility of their marriage to the man they happen to have set their hearts on, is only equalled by the alacrity with which they marry him when the time comes.

Having set Dick and Augusta down to a breakfast of porridge and coffee, which both of them thought delicious, though the fare was really rather coarse, Mrs. Thomas, being unable to restrain her curiosity, rowed off to the land to see the huts and also Mr. Meeson's remains, which, though not a pleasant sight, were undoubtedly an interesting one. With her, too, went most of the crew, bent upon the same errand, and also on obtaining water, of which the Harpoon was short.

As soon as she was left alone, Augusta went back to the cabin, taking Dick with her, and laid herself down on the berth with a feeling of safety and thankfulness to which she had long been a stranger, where very soon she fell sound asleep.

CHAPTER XII.
SOUTHAMPTON QUAY.

When Augusta opened her eyes again she became conscious of a violent rolling motion that she could not mistake. They were at sea.

She got up, smoothed her hair, and went on deck, to find that she had slept for many hours, for the sun was setting. She went aft to where Mrs. Thomas was sitting near the wheel with little Dick beside her, and after greeting them, turned to watch the sunset. The sight was a beautiful one enough, for the great waves, driven by the westerly wind, which in these latitudes is nearly always blowing half a gale, were rushing past them wild and free, and the sharp spray of their foaming crests struck upon her forehead like a whip. The sun was setting, and the arrows of the dying light flew fast and far across the billowy bosom of the deep. Fast and far they flew from the stormy glory in the west, lighting up the pale surfaces of cloud, and tinging the grey waters of that majestic sea with a lurid hue of blood. They kissed the bellying sails, and seemed to rest upon the vessel's lofty trucks, and then travelled on and away, and away, through the great empyrean of space till they broke and vanished upon the horizon's rounded edge. There behind them—miles behind—Kerguelen Land reared its fierce cliffs against the twilight sky. Clear and desolate they towered in an unutterable solitude, and on their snowy surfaces the sunbeams beat coldly as the warm breath of some human passion beating on Aphrodite's marble breast.

Augusta gazed upon those drear cliffs that had so nearly proved her monumental pile and shuddered. It was as a hideous dream.

And then the dark and creeping shadows of the night threw their veils around and over them, and they vanished. They were swallowed up in blackness, and she lost sight of them and of the great seas that forever beat and churn about their stony feet; nor except in dreams, did she again set her eyes upon their measureless solitude.

The Night arose in strength and shook a golden dew of stars from the tresses of her streaming clouds, till the wonderful deep heavens sparkled with a myriad gemmy points. The west wind going on his way sung his wild chant amongst the cordage, and rushed among the sails as with a rush of wings. The ship leant over like a maiden shrinking from a kiss, then, shivering, fled away, leaping from billow to billow as they rose and tossed their white arms about her, fain to drag her down and hold her to ocean's heaving breast.

The rigging tautened, and the huge sails flapped in thunder as the Harpoon sped upon her course, and all around was greatness and the present majesty of power. Augusta looked aloft and sighed, she knew not why. The swift blood of youth coursed through her veins, and she rejoiced exceedingly that life and all its possibilities yet lay before her. But a little more of that dreadful place and they would have lain behind. Her days would have been numbered before she scarce had time to strike a blow in the great human struggle that rages ceaselessly from age to age. The voice of her genius would have been hushed just as its notes began to thrill, and her message would never have been spoken in the world. But now Time was once more before her, and oh! the nearness of Death had taught her the unspeakable value of that one asset on which we can rely—Life. Not, indeed, that life for which so many live—the life led for self, and having for its principle, if not its only end, the gratification of the desires of self; but an altogether higher life—a life devoted to telling that which her keen instinct knew was truth, and, however imperfectly, painting with the pigment of her noble art those visions of beauty which sometimes seemed to rest like heavenly shadows on her soul.

Three months have passed—three long months of tossing waters and ever-present winds. The Harpoon, shaping her course for Norfolk, in the United States, had made but a poor passage of it. She got into the south-east trades, and all went well till they made St. Paul's Rocks, where they were detained by the doldrums and variable winds. Afterwards she passed into the north-east trades, and then, further north, met a series of westerly gales, that ultimately drove her to the Azores, just as her crew were getting very short of water and provisions. And here Augusta bid farewell to her friend the Yankee skipper; for the whaler that had saved her life and Dick's, after refitting once more, set sail upon its almost endless voyage. She stood on the breakwater at Ponta Delgada, and watched the Harpoon drop past. The men recognized her and cheered lustily, and Captain Thomas took off his hat; for the entire ship's company, down to the cabin-boy, were head-over-heels in love with Augusta; and the extraordinary offerings that they had made her on parting, most of them connected in some way or other with that noble animal the whale, sufficed to fill a good-sized packing-case. Augusta waved her handkerchief to them in answer; but she could not see much of them, because her eyes were full of tears. She had had quite enough of the Harpoon, and yet she was loth to say farewell to her; for her days on board had in many respects been restful and happy ones; they had given her space and time to brace herself up before she plunged once more into the struggle of active life. Besides, she had throughout been treated with that unvarying kindness and consideration for which the American people are justly noted in their dealings with all persons in misfortune.

But Augusta was not the only person who with sorrow watched the departure of the Harpoon. First, there was little Dick, who had acquired a fine Yankee drawl, and grown quite half an inch on board of her, and who fairly howled when his particular friend, a remarkably fierce and grisly-looking boatswain, brought him as a parting offering a large whale's tooth, patiently carved by himself with a spirited picture of their rescue on Kerguelen Land. Then there was Mrs. Thomas herself. When they finally reached the island of St. Michael, in the Azores, Augusta had offered to pay fifty pounds, being half of the hundred sovereigns given to her by Mr. Meeson, to Captain Thomas as a passage fee, knowing that he was by no moans overburdened with the goods of this world. But he stoutly declined to touch a farthing, saying that it would be unlucky to take money from a castaway. Augusta as stoutly insisted; and, finally, a compromise was come to. Mrs. Thomas was anxious, being seized with that acute species of home-sickness from which Suffolk people are no more exempt than other folk, to visit the land where she was born and the people midst whom she was bred up. But this she could not well afford to do. Therefore, Augusta's proffered fifty pounds was appropriated to this purpose, and Mrs. Thomas stopped with Augusta at Ponta Delgada, waiting for the London and West India Line Packet to take them to Southampton.

So it came to pass that they stood together on the Ponta Delgada breakwater and together saw the Harpoon sail off towards the setting sun.

Then came a soft dreamy fortnight in the fair island of St. Michael, where nature is ever as a bride, and never reaches the stage of the hard-worked, toil-worn mother, lank and lean with the burden of maternity. The mental act of looking back to this time, in after years, always recalled to Augusta's senses the odor of orange-blossoms, and the sight of the rich pomegranate-bloom blushing the roses down. It was a pleasant time, for the English Consul there most hospitably entertained them—with much more personal enthusiasm, indeed, than he generally considered it necessary to show towards shipwrecked voyagers—a class of people of whom consular representatives abroad must get rather tired with their eternal misfortunes and their perennial want of clothes. Indeed, the only drawback to her enjoyment was that the Consul, a gallant official, with red hair, equally charmed by her adventures, her literary fame, and her person, showed a decided disposition to fall in love with her, and a red-haired and therefore ardent Consular officer is, under those circumstances, a somewhat alarming personage. But the time went on without anything serious happening; and, at last, one morning after breakfast, a man came running up with the information that the mail was in sight.

And so Augusta took an affectionate farewell of the golden-haired Consul, who gazed at her through his eyeglass, and sighed when he thought of what might have been in the sweet by-and-by; and the ship's bell rang, and the screw began to turn, leaving the Consul still sighing on the horizon; and in due course Augusta and Mrs. Thomas found themselves standing on the quay at Southampton, the centre of an admiring and enthusiastic crowd.

The captain had told the extraordinary tale to the port officials when they boarded the vessel, and on getting ashore the port officials had made haste to tell every living soul they met the wonderful news that two survivors of the ill-fated Kangaroo—the history of whose tragic end had sent a thrill of horror through the English-speaking world—were safe and sound on board the West India boat. Thus, by the time that Augusta, Mrs. Thomas, and Dick were safe on shore, their story, or rather sundry distorted versions of it, was flashing up the wires to the various press agencies, and running through Southampton like wild-fire. Scarcely were their feet set upon the quay, when, with a rush and a bound, wild men, with note-books in their hands, sprang upon them, and beat them down with a rain of questions. Augusta found it impossible to answer them all at once, so contented herself with saying, "Yes," "Yes," "Yes," to everything, out of which mono-syllable, she afterwards found to her surprise, these fierce and active pressmen contrived to make up a sufficiently moving tale; which included glowing accounts of the horrors of the shipwreck, and, what rather took her aback, a positive statement that she and the sailors had lived for a fortnight upon the broiled remains of Mr. Meeson. One interviewer, being a small man, and, therefore, unable to kick and fight his way through the ring which surrounded Augusta and Mrs. Thomas, seized upon little Dick, and commenced to chirp and snap his fingers at him in the intervals of asking him such questions as he thought suitable to his years.

Dick, dreadfully alarmed, fled with a howl; but this did not prevent a column and a half of matter, headed "The Infant's Tale of Woe," from appearing that very day in a journal noted for the accuracy and unsensational character of its communications. Nor was the army of interviewers the only terror that they had to face. Little girls gave them bouquets; an old lady, whose brain was permeated with the idea that shipwrecked people went about in a condition of undress for much longer than was necessary after the event, arrived with an armful of under-clothing streaming on the breeze; and last, but not least, a tall gentleman, with a beautiful moustache, thrust into Augusta's hand a note hastily written in pencil, which, when opened, proved to be an *offer of marriage*!

However, at last they found themselves in a first-class carriage, ready to start, or rather starting. The interviewing gentlemen, two of whom had their heads jammed through the window, were forcibly drawn away—still asking questions, by the officials—the tall gentleman with the moustache, who was hovering in the background, smiled a soft farewell, in which modesty struggled visibly with hope, the station-master took off his cap, and in another minute they were rolling out of Southampton Station.

Augusta sank back with a sigh of relief, and then burst out laughing at the thought of the gentleman with the fair moustachios. On the seat opposite to her somebody had thoughtfully placed a number of the day's papers. She took up the first that came to hand and glanced at it idly with the idea of trying to pick up the thread of events. Her eyes fell instantly upon the name of Mr. Gladstone printed all over the sheet in type of varying size, and she sighed. Life on the ocean wave had been perilous and disagreeable enough, but at any rate she had been free from Mr. Gladstone and his doings. Whatever evil might be said of him, he was *not* an old man of the sea. Turning the paper over impatiently she came upon the reports of the Probate Divorce and Admiralty Division of the High Court. The first report ran thus:—

BEFORE THE RIGHT HONOURABLE THE PRESIDENT.

IN THE MATTER OF MEESON, DECEASED.

This was an application arising out of the loss of R.M.S. Kangaroo, on the eighteenth of December last. It will be remembered that out of about a thousand souls on board that vessel the occupants of one boat only—twenty-five people in all—were saved. Among the drowned was Mr. Meeson, the head of the well-known Birmingham publishing company of Meeson, Addison, and Roscoe, and Co. (Limited), who was at the time on a visit to New Zealand and Australia in connection with the business of the company.

Mr. Fiddlestick, Q.C., who with Mr. Pearl appeared for the applicants (and who was somewhat imperfectly heard), stated that the facts connected with the sinking of the Kangaroo would probably still be so fresh in his Lordship's mind that it would not be necessary for him to detail them, although he had them upon affidavit before him. His Lordship would remember that but one boat-load of people had survived from this, perhaps the most terrible shipwreck of the generation. Among the drowned was Mr. Meeson; and this application was on behalf of the executors of his will for leave to presume his death. The property which passed under the will was very large indeed; amounting in all, Mr. Fiddlestick understood, to about two millions sterling, which, perhaps, might incline his Lordship to proceed very carefully in allowing probate to issue.

The President: Well—the amount of the property has got nothing to do with the principles on which the Court acts with regard to the presumption of death, Mr. Fiddlestick.

Quite so, my Lord, and I think that in this case your Lordship will be satisfied that there is no reason why probate should not issue. It is, humanly speaking, impossible that Mr. Meeson can have escaped the general destruction.

The President: Have you any affidavit from anybody who saw Mr. Meeson in the water?

No, my Lord; I have an affidavit from a sailor named Okers, the only man who was picked up in the water after the Kangaroo foundered, which states that he believes that he saw Mr. Meeson spring from the ship into the water, but the affidavit does not carry the matter further. He cannot swear that it was Mr. Meeson.

The President: Well, I think that that will do. The Court is necessarily adverse to allowing the presumption of death, except on evidence of the most satisfactory nature. Still, considering that nearly four months have now passed since the foundering of the Kangaroo under circumstances which make it exceedingly improbable that there were any other survivors, I think that it may fairly presume that Mr. Meeson shared the fate of the other passengers.

Mr. Fiddlestick: The death to be presumed from the 18th of December.

The President: Yes, from the eighteenth.

Mr. Fiddlestick: If your Lordship pleases.

Augusta put down the paper with a gasp. There was she, safe and sound, with the true last will of Mr. Meeson tattooed upon her; and "probate had issued"—whatever that mysterious formula might mean—to another will, not the real last will. It meant (as she in her ignorance supposed) that her will was no good, that she had endured that abominable tattooing to no purpose, and was, to no purpose, scarred for life.

It was too much; and, in a fit of vexation, she flung the *Times* out of the window, and cast herself back on the cushion, feeling very much inclined to cry.

CHAPTER XIII.
EUSTACE BUYS A PAPER.

In due course the train that bore Augusta and her fortunes, timed to reach Waterloo at 5.40 p.m., rolled into the station. The train was a fast one, but the telegraph had been faster. All the evening papers had come out with accounts, more or less accurate, of their escape, and most of them had added that the two survivors would reach Waterloo by the 5.40 train. The consequence was, that when the train drew up at the platform, Augusta, on looking out, was horrified to see a dense mass of human beings being kept in check by a line of policemen.

However, the guard was holding the door open, so there was nothing for it but to get out, which she did, taking Dick by the hand, a proceeding that necessarily put her identity beyond a doubt. The moment she got her foot on to the platform, the crowd saw her, and there arose such a tremendous shout of welcome that she very nearly took refuge again in the carriage. For a moment she stood hesitating, and the crowd, seeing how sweet and beautiful she was (for the three months of sea air had made her stouter and even more lovely), cheered again with that peculiar enthusiasm which a discerning public always shows for a pretty face. But even while she stood bewildered on the platform she heard a loud "Make way—make way there!" and saw the multitude being divided by a little knot of officials, who were escorting somebody dressed in widow's weeds.

In another second there was a cry of joy, and a sweet, pale faced little lady had run at the child Dick, and was hugging him against her heart, and sobbing and laughing both at once.

"Oh! my boy! my boy!" cried Lady Holmhurst, for it was she, "I thought you were dead—long ago dead!"

And then she turned, and, before all the people there, clung about Augusta's neck and kissed her and blessed her, because she had saved her only child, and half removed the deadweight of her desolation. Whereat the crowd cheered, and wept, and yelled, and swore with excitement, and blessed their stars that they were there to see.

And then, in a haze of noise and excitement, they were led through the cheering mob to where a carriage and pair were standing, and were helped into it, Mrs. Thomas being placed on the front seat, and Lady Holmhurst and Augusta on the back, the former with the gasping Dick upon her knee.

And now little Dick is out of the story.

Then another event occurred, which we must go back a little to explain.

When Eustace Meeson had come to town, after being formally disinherited, he had managed to get a billet as Latin, French, and Old English reader in a publishing house of repute. As it happened, on this very afternoon he was strolling down the Strand, having finished a rather stiff day's work, and with a mind filled with those idle and somewhat confused odds and ends of speculation with which most brain workers will be acquainted. He looked older and paler than when we last met him, for sorrow and misfortune had laid their heavy hands upon him. When Augusta had departed, he had discovered that he was head over heels in love with her in that unfortunate way—for ninety-nine times out of a hundred, it is unfortunate—in which many men of susceptibility do occasionally fall in love in their youth—a way that brands the heart for life in a fashion that can no more be effaced than the stamp of a hot iron can be effaced from the physical body. Such an affection—which is not altogether of the earth—will, when it overcomes a man, prove either the greatest blessing of his life or one of the heaviest, most enduring curses that a malignant fate can heap upon his head. For if he achieves his desire, even though he serve his seven years, surely for him life will be robbed of half its evil. But if he lose her, either through misfortune or because he gave all this to one who did not understand the gift, or one who looked at love and on herself as a currency wherewith to buy her place and the luxury of days, then he will be of all men among the most miserable. For nothing can give him back that which has gone from him.

Eustace had never seen Augusta but twice in his life; but then passion does not necessarily depend upon constant previous intercourse with its object. Love at first sight is common enough, and in this instance Eustace was not altogether dependent upon the spoken words of his adored, or on his recollection of her very palpable beauty. For he had her books. To those who know something of the writer—sufficient, let us say, to enable him to put an approximate value on his or her sentiments, so as to form a more or less accurate guess as to when he is speaking from his own mind, when he is speaking from the mind of the puppet in hand, and when he is merely putting a case—a person's books are full of information, and bring that person into a closer and more intimate contact with the reader than any amount of personal intercourse. For whatever is best and whatever is worst in an individual will be reflected in his pages, seeing that, unless he is the poorest of hack authors, he must of necessity set down therein the images that pass across the mirrors of his heart.

Thus it seemed to Eustace, who knew "Jemima's Vow" and also her previous abortive work almost by heart, that he was very intimately acquainted with Augusta, and as he was walking home that May evening, he was reflecting sadly enough of all that he had lost through that cruel shipwreck. He had lost Augusta, and, what was more, he had lost his uncle and his uncle's vast fortune. For he, too, had seen the report of the application re Meeson in the *Times*, and, though he knew that he was disinherited, it was a little crushing. He had lost the fortune for Augusta's sake, and now he had lost Augusta also; and he reflected, not without dismay, on the long dreary existence that stretched away before him, filled up as it were with prospective piles of Latin proofs. With a sigh he halted at the Wellington-street crossing in the Strand, which, owing to the constant stream of traffic at this point, is one of the worst in London. There was a block at the moment, as there generally is, and he stood for some minutes watching the frantic dashes of an old woman, who always tried to cross it at the wrong time, not without some amusement. Presently, however, a boy with a bundle of unfolded *Globes* under his arm came rushing along, making the place hideous with his howls.

"Wonderful escape of a lady and han infant!" he roared. "Account of the survivors of the Kangaroo—wonderful escape—desert island—arrival of the Magnolia with the criminals."

Eustace jumped, and instantly bought a copy of the paper, stepping into the doorway of a shop where they sold masonic jewels of every size and hue, in order to read it. The very first thing that his eye fell on was an editorial paragraph.

"In another column," ran the paragraph, "will be found a short account, telegraphed to us from Southampton just as we are going to press, of the most remarkable tale of the sea that we are acquainted with. The escape of Miss Augusta Smithers and of the little Lord Holmhurst—as we suppose that we must now call him—from the ill-fated Kangaroo, and their subsequent rescue, on Kerguelen Land, by the American whaler, will certainly take rank as the most romantic incident of its kind in the recent annals of shipwreck. Miss Smithers, who will be better known to the public as the authoress of that charming book 'Jemima's Vow,' which took the town by storm about a year ago, will arrive at Waterloo Station by the 5.40 train, and we shall then—"

Eustace read no more. Sick and faint with an extraordinary revulsion of feeling, he leant against the door of the masonic shop, which promptly opened in the most hospitable manner, depositing him upon his back on the floor of the establishment. In a second he was up, and had bounded out of the shop with such energy that the shopman was on the point of holloaing "Stop thief!" It was exactly five o'clock, and he was not more than a quarter of a mile or so from Waterloo Station. A hansom was sauntering along in front of him, he sprang into it. "Waterloo, main line," he shouted, "as hard as you can go," and in another moment he was rolling across the bridge. Five or six minutes' drive brought him to the station, to which an enormous number of people were hurrying, collected together partly by a rumour of what was going on, and partly by that magnetic contagion of excitement which runs through a London mob like fire through dry grass.

He dismissed the hansom, throwing the driver half-a-crown, which, considering that half-crowns were none too plentiful with him, was a rash thing to do, and vigorously shouldered his way through the crush till he reached the spot where the carriage and pair were standing. The carriage was just beginning to move on.

"Stop!" he shouted at the top of his voice to the coachman, who pulled up again. In another moment he was alongside, and there, sweeter and more beautiful than ever, he once more saw his love.

She started at his voice, which she seemed to know, and their eyes met. Their eyes met and a great light of happiness shot into her sweet face and shone there till it was covered up and lost in the warm blush that followed.

He tried to speak, but could not. Twice he tried, and twice he failed, and meanwhile the mob shouted like anything. At last, however, he got it out— "Thank God!" he stammered, "thank God you are safe!"

For answer, she stretched out her hand and gave him one sweet look. He took it, and once more the carriage began to move on.

"Where are you to be found?" he had the presence of mind to ask.

"At Lady Holmhurst's. Come to-morrow morning; I have something to tell you," she answered, and in another minute the carriage was gone, leaving him standing there in a condition of mind which really "can be better imagined than described."

CHAPTER XIV.
AT HANOVER-SQUARE.

Eustace could never quite remember how he got through the evening of that eventful day. Everything connected with it seemed hazy to him. As, however, fortunately for the reader of this history, we are not altogether dependent on the memory of a young man in love, which is always a treacherous thing to deal with, having other and exclusive sources of information, we may as well fill the gap. First of all he went to his club and seized a "Red-book," in which he discovered that Lord Holmhurst's, or, rather, Lady Holmhurst's, London house was in Hanover-square. Then he walked to his rooms in one of the little side-streets opening out of the Strand, and went through the form of eating some dinner; after which a terrible fit of restlessness got possession of him, and he started out walking. For three solid hours did that young man walk, which was, no doubt, a good thing for him, for one never gets enough exercise in London; and at the end of that time, having already been to Hammersmith and back, he found himself gravitating towards Hanover-square. Once there, he had little difficulty in finding the number. There was a light in the drawing-room floor, and, the night being warm, one of the windows was open, so that the lamp-light shone softly through the lace curtains. Eustace crossed over to the other side of the street, and, leaning against the iron railings of the square, looked up. He was rewarded for his pains, for, through the filmy curtain, he could make out the forms of two ladies, seated side by side upon an ottoman, with their faces towards the window, and in one of these he had no difficulty in recognising Augusta. Her head was leaning on her hand, and she was talking earnestly to her companion. He wondered what she was talking of, and had half a mind to go and ring, and ask to see her. Why should he wait till to-morrow morning? Presently, however, better counsels prevailed, and, though sorely against his will, he stopped where he was till a policeman, thinking his rapt gaze suspicious, gruffly requested him to move on.

To gaze at one's only love through an open window is, no doubt, a delightful occupation, if a somewhat tantalising one; but if Eustace's ears had been as good as his eyes, and he could have heard the conversation that was proceeding in the drawing-room, he would have been still more interested.

Augusta had just been unfolding that part of her story which dealt with the important document tattooed upon her shoulders, to which Lady Holmhurst had listened "ore rotundo."

"And so the young man is coming here to-morrow morning," said Lady Holmhurst; "how delightful! I am sure he looked a very nice young man, and he had very fine eyes. It is the most romantic thing that I ever heard of."

"It may be delightful for you, Bessie," said Augusta, rather tartly, "but I call it disgusting. It is all very well to be tattooed upon a desert island—not that that was very nice, I can tell you; but it is quite another thing to have to show the results in a London drawing-room. Of course, Mr. Meeson will want to see this will, whatever it may be worth; and I should like to ask you, Bessie, how I am to show it to him? It is on my neck."

"I have not observed," said Lady Holmhurst, drily, "that ladies, as a rule, have an insuperable objection to showing their necks. If you have any doubt on the point, I recommend you to get an invitation to a London ball. All you will have to do will be to wear a low dress. The fact of being tattooed does not make it any more improper for you to show your shoulders, than it would be if they were not tattooed."

"I have never worn a low dress," said Augusta, "and I do not want to show my shoulders."

"Ah, well," said Lady Holmhurst, darkly; "I daresay that that feeling will soon wear off. But, of course, if you won't, you won't; and, under those circumstances, you had better say nothing about the will—though," she added learnedly, "of course that would be compounding a felony."

"Would it? I don't quite see where the felony comes in."

"Well, of course, it is this way: you steal the will—that's felony; and if you don't show it to him, I suppose you compound it; it is a double offence—compound felony."

"Nonsense!" answered Augusta to this exposition of the law, which was, it will be admitted, almost as lucid and convincing as that of an average Q.C. "How can I steal my own shoulders? It is impossible."

"Oh, no; not at all. You don't know what funny things you can do. I once had a cousin whom I coached for his examination for the Bar, and I learnt a great deal about it then. Poor fellow! he was plucked eight times."

"I am sure I don't wonder at it," said Augusta, rudely. "Well, I suppose I must put on this low dress; but it is horrid—perfectly horrid! You will have to lend me one, that is all."

"My dear," answered Lady Holmhurst, with a glance at her widow's weeds. "I have no low dresses: though, perhaps, I can find some among the things I put away before we sailed," and her eyes filled with tears.

Augusta took her hand, and they began to talk of that great bereavement and of their own wonderful survival, till at last she led the conversation round to little Dick, and Bessie Holmhurst smiled again at the thought that her darling boy, her only child, was safe asleep up stairs, and not, as she had believed, washing to and fro at the bottom of the ocean. She took Augusta's hand and kissed it, and blessed her for having saved her child, till suddenly, somewhat to the relief of the latter, the butler opened the door and said that two gentlemen wanted very particularly to speak to Miss Smithers. And then she was once more handed over to her old enemies, the interviewers; and after them came the representatives of the company, and then more special reporters, and then an artist from one of the illustrated papers, who insisted upon her giving him an appointment in language that, though polite, indicated that he meant to have his way; and so on till nearly midnight, when she rushed off to bed and locked her door.

Next morning Augusta appeared at breakfast dressed in an exceedingly becoming low dress, which Lady Holmhurst sent up to her with her hot water. She had never worn one before, and it certainly is trying to put on a low dress for the first time in full daylight—indeed, she felt as guilty as does a person of temperate habits when he is persuaded to drink a brandy and soda before getting up. However, there was no help for it; so, throwing a shawl over her shoulders, she descended.

"My dear, do let me see," said Lady Holmhurst, as soon as the servant had left the room.

With a sigh Augusta uncovered her shoulders, and her friend ran round the table to look at them. There, on her neck, was the will. The cuttle ink had proved an excellent medium, and the tattooing was as fresh as the day on which it had been done, and would, no doubt, remain so till the last hour of her life.

"Well," said Lady Holmhurst, "I hope the young man will be duly grateful. I should have to be very much in love," and she looked meaningly at Augusta, "before I would spoil myself in that fashion for any man."

Augusta blushed at the insinuation, and said nothing. At ten o'clock, just as they were half through breakfast, there came a ring at the bell.

"Here he is," said Lady Holmhurst, clapping her hands. "Well, if this isn't the very funniest thing that I ever heard of! I told Jones to show him in here."

Hardly were the words out of her mouth when the butler, who looked as solemn as a mute in his deep mourning, opened the door and announced "Mr. Eustace Meeson," in those deep and commanding tones which flunkeys, and flunkeys alone, have at their command. There was a moment's pause. Augusta half rose from her chair, and then sat down again; and, noticing her embarrassment, Lady Holmhurst smiled maliciously. Then came in Eustace himself, looking rather handsome, exceedingly nervous, and beautifully got up—in a frock-coat, with a flower in it.

"Oh! how do you do?" he said to Augusta, holding out his hand, which she took rather coldly.

"How do you do, Mr. Meeson," she answered. "Let me introduce you to Lady Holmhurst. Mr. Meeson, Lady Holmhurst." Eustace bowed, and put his hat down on the butter-dish, for he was very much overcome.

"I hope that I have not come too early," he said in great confusion, as he perceived his mistake. "I thought that you would have done breakfast."

"Oh, not at all Mr. Meeson," said Lady Holmhurst. "Won't you have a cup of tea? Augusta, give Mr. Meeson a cup of tea."

He took the tea, which he did not want in the least, and then there came an awkward silence. Nobody seemed to know how to begin the conversation.

"How did you find the house, Mr. Meeson?" said Lady Holmhurst, at last. "Miss Smithers gave you no address, and there are two Lady Holmhursts—my mother-in-law and myself."

"Oh, I looked it out, and then I walked here last night and saw you both sitting at the window."

"Indeed!" said Lady Holmhurst. "And why did you not come in? You might have helped to protect Miss Smithers from the reporters."

"I don't know," he answered confusedly. "I did not like to; and, besides, a policeman thought I was a suspicious character and told me to move on."

"Dear me, Mr. Meeson; you must have been having a good look at us."

Here Augusta interposed, fearing lest her admirer—for with an unerring instinct, she now guessed how matters stood—should say something foolish. A young man who is capable of standing to stare at a house in Hanover-square is, she thought, evidently capable of anything.

"I was surprised to see you yesterday," she said. "How did you know we were coming?"

Eustace told her that he had seen it in the *Globe.* "I am sure you cannot have been so surprised as I was," he went on, "I had made sure that you were drowned. I went up to Birmingham to call on you after you had gone, and found that you had vanished and left no address. The maid-servant declared that you had sailed in a ship called the 'Conger Eel'—which I afterwards found out was Kangaroo. And then she went down; and after a long time they published a full list of the passengers and your name was not among them, and I thought that after all you might have got off the ship or something. Then, some days afterwards, came a telegram from Albany, in Australia, giving the names of Lady Holmhurst and the others who were saved, and specially mentioning 'Miss Smithers—the novelist' and Lord Holmhurst as being among the drowned, and that is how the dreadful suspense came to an end. It was awful, I can tell you."

Both of the young women looked at Eustace's face and saw that there was no mistaking the real nature of the trial through which he had passed. So real was it, that it never seemed to occur to him that there was anything unusual in his expressing such intense interest in the affairs of a young lady with whom he was outwardly, at any rate, on the terms of merest acquaintance.

"It was very kind of you to think so much about me," said Augusta, gently. "I had no idea that you would call again, or I would have left word where I was going."

"Well, thank God you are safe and sound, at any rate," answered Eustace; and then, with a sudden burst of anxiety, "you are not going back to New Zealand just yet, are you?"

"I don't know. I am rather sick of the sea just now."

"No, indeed, she is not," said Lady Holmhurst; "she is going to stop with me and Dick. Miss Smithers saved Dick's life, you know, when the nurse, poor thing, had run away. And now, dear, you had better tell Mr. Meeson about the will."

"The will. What will?" asked Eustace.

"Listen, and you will hear."

And Eustace did listen with open eyes and ears while Augusta, getting over her shyness as best she might, told the whole story of his uncle's death, and of the way in which he had communicated his testamentary wishes.

"And do you mean to tell me," said Eustace, astounded, "that you allowed him to have his confounded will tattooed upon your neck?"

"Yes," answered Augusta, "I did; and what is more, Mr. Meeson, I think that you ought to be very much obliged to me; for I daresay that I shall often be sorry for it."

"I am *very* much obliged," answered Eustace; "I had no right to expect such a thing, and, in short, I do not know what to say. I should never have thought that any woman was capable of such a sacrifice for—for a comparative stranger."

Then came another awkward pause.

"Well, Mr. Meeson," said Augusta, at last rising brusquely from her chair, "the document belongs to you, and so I suppose that you had better see it. Not that I think that it will be of much use to you, however, as I see that 'probate had been allowed to issue,' whatever that may mean, of Mr. Meeson's other will."

"I do not know that that will matter," said Eustace, "as I heard a friend of mine, Mr. Short, who is a barrister, talk about some case the other day in which probate was revoked on the production of a subsequent will."

"Indeed!" answered Augusta, "I am very glad to hear that. Then, perhaps, after all I have been tattooed to some purpose. Well; I suppose you had better see it," and with a gesture that was half shy and half defiant she drew the lace shawl from her shoulders, and turned her back towards him so that he might see what was inscribed across it.

Eustace stared at the broad line of letters which with the signatures written underneath might mean a matter of two millions of money to him.

"Thank you," he said at last, and, taking up the lace shawl, he threw it over her again.

"If you will excuse me for a few minutes, Mr. Meeson," interrupted Lady Holmhurst at this point; "I have to go to see about the dinner," and before Augusta could interfere she had left the room.

Eustace closed the door behind her, and turned, feeling instinctively that a great crisis in his fortunes had come. There are some men who rise to an emergency and some who shrink from it, and the difference is, that difference between him who succeeds and him who fails in life, and in all that makes life worth living.

Eustace belonged to the class that rises and not to that which shrinks.

CHAPTER XV.
EUSTACE CONSULTS A LAWYER.

Augusta was leaning against the marble mantelpiece—indeed, one of her arms was resting upon it, for she was a tall woman. Perhaps she, too, felt that there was something in the air; at any rate, she turned away her head, and began to play with a bronze Japanese lobster which adorned the mantelpiece.

"Now for it," said Eustace to himself, drawing a long breath, to try and steady the violent pulsations of his heart.

"I don't know what to say to you, Miss Smithers," he began.

"Best say nothing more about it," she put in quickly. "I did it, and I am glad that I did it. What do a few marks matter if a great wrong is prevented thereby? I am not ever likely to have to go to court. Besides, Mr. Meeson, there is another thing; it was through me that you lost your inheritance; it is only right that I should try to be the means of bringing it back to you."

She dropped her head again, and once more began to play with the bronze lobster, holding her arm in such a fashion that Eustace could not see her face. But if he could not see her face she could see his in the glass, and narrowly observed its every change, which, on the whole, though natural, was rather mean of her.

Poor Eustace grew pale and paler yet, till his handsome countenance became positively ghastly. It is wonderful how frightened young men are the first time that they propose. It wears off afterwards—with practice one gets accustomed to anything.

"Miss Smithers—Augusta," he gasped, "I want to say something to you!" and he stopped dead.

"Yes, Mr. Meeson," she answered cheerfully, "what is it?"

"I want to tell you"—and again he hesitated.

"What you are going to do about the will?" suggested Augusta.

"No—no; nothing about the will—please don't laugh at me and put me off!"

She looked up innocently—as much as to say that she never dreamed of doing either of these things. She had a lovely face, and the glance of the grey eyes quite broke down the barrier of his fears.

"Oh, Augusta, Augusta," he said, "don't you understand? I love you! I love you! No woman was ever loved before as I love you. I fell in love with you the very first time I saw you in the office at Meeson's, when I had the row with my uncle about you; and ever since then I have got deeper and deeper in love with you. When I thought that you were drowned it nearly broke my heart, and often and often I wished that I were dead, too!"

It was Augusta's turn to be disturbed now, for, though a lady's composure will stand her in good stead up to the very verge of an affair of this sort, it generally breaks down *in medias res*. Anyhow, she certainly dropped her eyes and colored to her hair, while her breast began to heave tumultuously.

"Do you know, Mr. Meeson," she said at last, without daring to look at his imploring face, "that this is only the fourth time that we have seen each other, including yesterday."

"Yes, I know," he said; "but don't refuse me on that account; you can see me as often as you like"—(this was generous of Master Eustace)—"and really I know you better than you think. I should think that I have read each of your books twenty times."

This was a happy stroke, for, however free from vanity a person may be, it is not in the nature of a young woman to hear that somebody has read her book twenty times without being pleased.

"I am not my books," said Augusta.

"No; but your books are part of you," he answered, "and I have learnt more about your real self through them than I should have done if I had seen you a hundred times instead of four."

Augusta slowly raised her grey eyes till they met his own, and looked at him as though she were searching out his soul, and the memory of that long, sweet look is with him yet.

He said no more, nor had she any words; but somehow nearer and nearer they drew one to the other, till his arms were around her, and his lips were pressed upon her lips. Happy man and happy girl! they will live to find that life has joys (for those who are good and are well off) but that it has no joys so holy and so complete as that which they were now experiencing—the first kiss of true and honest love.

A little while afterwards the butler came in in a horribly sudden manner, and found Augusta and Eustace, the one very red and the other very pale, standing suspiciously close to each other. But he was a very well-trained butler and a man of experience, who had seen much and guessed more; and he looked innocent as a babe unborn.

Just then, too, Lady Holmhurst came in again and looked at the pair of them with an amused twinkle in her eye. Lady Holmhurst, like her butler, was also a person of experience.

"Won't you come into the drawing room?" she said. And they did, looking rather sheepish.

And there Eustace made a clean breast of it, announcing that they were engaged to be married. And although this was somewhat of an assumption, seeing that no actual words of troth had passed between them, Augusta stood there, never offering a word in contradiction.

"Well, Mr. Meeson," said Lady Holmhurst, "I think that you are the luckiest man of my acquaintance, for Augusta is not only one of the sweetest and loveliest girls that I have ever met, she is also the bravest and the cleverest. You will have to look out, Mr. Meeson, or you will be known as the husband of the great Augusta Meeson."

"I will take the risk," he answered humbly. "I know that Augusta has more brains in her little finger than I have in my whole body. I don't know how she can look at a fellow like me."

"Dear me, how humble we are!" said Lady Holmhurst. "Well, that is the way of men before marriage. And now, as Augusta carries both your fortunes on her back as well as in her face and brain, I venture to suggest that you had better go and see a lawyer about the matter; that is, if you have quite finished your little talk. I suppose that you will come and dine with us, Mr. Meeson, and if you like to come a little early, say half-past six, I daresay that Augusta will arrange to be in, to hear what you have found out about this will, you know. And now—au revoir."

"I think that that is a very nice young man, my dear," said Lady Holmhurst as soon as Eustace had bowed himself out. "It was rather audacious of him to propose to you the fourth time that he set eyes upon you; but I think that audacity is, on the whole, a good quality in the male sex. Another thing is, that if that will is worth anything he will be one of the wealthiest men in the whole of England; so, taking it altogether, I think I may congratulate you, my dear. And now I suppose that you have been in love with this young man all along. I guessed as much when I saw your face as he ran up to the carriage yesterday, and I was sure of it when I heard about the tattooing. No girl would allow herself to be tattooed in the interest of abstract justice. Oh, yes! I know all about it; and now I am going out walking in the park with Dick, and I should advise you to compose yourself, for that artist is coming to draw you at twelve."

And she departed and left Augusta to her reflections, which were—well, not unpleasant ones.

Meanwhile Eustace was marching towards the Temple. As it happened, in the same lodging-house where he had been living for the last few months, two brothers of the name of Short had rooms, and with these young gentlemen he had become very friendly. The two Shorts were twins, and so like one another that it was more than a month before Eustace could be sure which of them he was speaking to. When they were both at college their father died, leaving his property equally between them; and as this property on realisation was not found to amount to more than four hundred a year, the twins very rightly concluded that they had better do something to supplement their moderate income. Accordingly, by a stroke of genius they determined that one of them should become a solicitor and the other a barrister, and then tossed up as to which should take to which trade. The idea, of course, was that in this manner they would be able to afford each other mutual comfort and support. John would give James briefs, and James' reflected glory would shine back on John. In short, they were anxious to establish a legal long firm of the most approved pattern.

Accordingly, they passed their respective examinations, and John took rooms with another budding solicitor in the City, while James hired chambers in Pump-court. But there the matter stopped, for as John did not get any work, of course he could not give any to James. And so it came to pass that for the past three years neither of the twins had found the law as profitable as they anticipated. In vain did John sit and sigh in the City. Clients were few and far between: scarcely enough to pay his rent. And in vain did James, artistically robed, wander like the Evil One, from court to court, seeking what he might devour. Occasionally he had the pleasure of taking a note for another barrister who was called away, which means doing another man's work for nothing. Once, too, a man with whom he had a nodding acquaintance, rushed up to him, and, thrusting a brief into his hands, asked him to hold it for him, telling him that it would be on in a short time, and that there was nothing in it—"nothing at all." Scarcely had poor James struggled through the brief when the case was called on, and it may suffice to say that at its conclusion, the Judge gazed at him mildly, over his spectacles, and "could not help wondering that any learned counsel had been found who would consent to waste the time of the Court in such a case as the one to which he had been listening." Clearly James' friend would not so consent, and had passed on the responsibility, minus the fee. On another occasion, James was in the Probate Court on motion day, and a solicitor—a real live solicitor—came up to him and asked him to make a motion (marked Mr.——, 2 gns.) for leave to dispense with a co-respondent. This motion he made, and the co-respondent was dispensed with in the approved fashion; but when he turned round the solicitor had vanished, and he never saw him more or the two guineas either. However, the brief, his only one, remained, and, after that, he took to hovering about the Divorce Court, partly in the hope of once more seeing that solicitor, and partly with a vague idea of drifting into practice in the Division.

Now, Eustace had often, when in the Shorts' sitting-room in the lodging-house in the Strand, heard the barrister James hold forth learnedly on the matter of wills, and, therefore, he naturally enough turned towards him in his recent dilemma. Knowing the address of his chambers in Pump-court, he hurried thither, and was in due course admitted by a very small child, who apparently filled the responsible office of clerk to Mr. James Short and several other learned gentlemen, whose names appeared upon the door.

The infant regarded Eustace, when he opened the door, with a look of such preternatural sharpness, that it almost frightened him. The beginning of that eagle glance was full of inquiring hope, and the end of resigned despair. The child had thought that Eustace might be a client come to tread the paths which no client ever had trod. Hence the hope and the despair in his eyes. Eustace had nothing of the solicitor's clerk about him. Clearly he was not a client.

Mr. Short was in "that door to the right." Eustace knocked, and entered into a bare little chamber about the size of a large housemaid's closet, furnished with a table, three chairs (one a basket easy), and a book-case, with a couple of dozen of law books, and some old volumes of reports, and a broad window-sill, in the exact centre of which lay the solitary and venerated brief.

Mr. James Short was a short, stout young man, with black eyes, a hooked nose, and a prematurely bald head. Indeed, this baldness of the head was the only distinguishing mark between James and John, and, therefore, a thing to be thankful for, though, of course, useless to the perplexed acquaintance who met them in the street when their hats were on. At the moment of Eustace's entry Mr. Short had been engaged in studying that intensely legal print, the *Sporting Times*, which, however, from some unexplained bashfulness, he had hastily thrown under the table, filling its space with a law book snatched at hazard from the shelf.

"All right, old fellow," said Eustace, whose quick eyes had caught the quick flutter of the vanishing paper; "don't be alarmed, it's only me."

"Ah!" said Mr. James Short, when he had shaken hands with him, "you see I thought that it might have been a client—a client is always possible, however improbable, and one has to be ready to meet the possibility."

"Quite so, old fellow," said Eustace; "but do you know, as it happens, I am a client—and a big one, too; it is a matter of two millions of money—my uncle's fortune. There was another will, and I want to take your advice."

Mr. Short fairly bounded out of the chair in exultation, and then, struck by another thought, sank back into it again.

"My dear Meeson," he said, "I am sorry I cannot hear you."

"Eh," said Eustace; "what do you mean?"

"I mean that you are not accompanied by a solicitor, and it is not the etiquette of the profession to which I belong to see a client unaccompanied by a solicitor."

"Oh, hang the etiquette of the profession!"

"My dear Meeson, if you came to me as a friend I should be happy to give you any legal information in my power, and I flatter myself that I know something of matters connected with probate. But you yourself said that you have come as a client, and in that case the personal relationship sinks into the background and is superseded by the official relationship. Under these circumstances it is evident that the etiquette of the profession intervenes, which overmastering force compels me to point out to you how improper and contrary to precedent it would be for me to listen to you without the presence of a properly qualified solicitor."

"Oh, Lord!" gasped Eustace, "I had no idea that you were so particular; I thought perhaps that you would be glad of the job."

"Certainly—certainly! In the present state of my practice," as he glanced at the solitary brief, "I should be the last to wish to turn away work. Let me suggest that you should go and consult my brother John, in the Poultry. I believe business is rather slack with him just now, so I think it probable that you will find him disengaged. Indeed, I dare say that I may go so far as to make an appointment for him here—let us say in an hour's time. Stop! I will consult my clerk! Dick!"

The infant appeared.

"I believe that I have no appointment for this morning?"

"No, Sir," said Dick, with a twinkle in his eye. "One moment, Sir, I will consult the book," and he vanished, to return presently with the information that Mr. Short's time was not under any contributions that day.

"Very good," said Mr. Short; "then make an entry of an appointment with Mr. John Short and Mr. Meeson, at two precisely."

"Yes, Sir," said Dick, departing to the unaccustomed task.

As soon as Eustace had departed from Tweedledum to Tweedledee, or, in other words, from James, barrister, to John, solicitor, Dick was again summoned and bade go to a certain Mr. Thomson on the next floor. Mr. Thomson had an excellent library, which had come to him by will. On the strength of this bequest, he had become a barrister-at-law, and the object of Dick's visit was to request the loan of the eighth volume of the statutes revised, containing the Wills Act of 1 Vic., cap. 26, "Brown on Probate,"

"Dixon on Probate," and "Powles on Brown," to the study of which valuable books Mr. James Short devoted himself earnestly whilst awaiting his client's return.

Meanwhile, Eustace had made his way in a two-penny 'bus to one of those busy courts in the City where Mr. John Short practised as a solicitor. Mr. Short's office was, Eustace discovered by referring to a notice board, on the seventh floor of one of the tallest houses he had ever seen. However, up he went with a stout heart, and after some five minutes of a struggle, that reminded him forcibly of climbing the ladders of a Cornish mine, he arrived at a little door right at the very top of the house on which was painted "Mr. John Short, solicitor." Eustace knocked and the door was opened by a small boy, so like the small boy he had seen at Mr. James Short's at the temple that he fairly started. Afterwards the mystery was explained. Like their masters, the two small boys were brothers.

Mr. John Short was within, and Eustace was ushered into his presence. To all appearance he was consulting a voluminous mass of correspondence written on large sheets of brief paper; but when he looked at it closely, it seemed to Eustace that the edges of the paper were very yellow, and the ink was much faded. This, however, was not to be wondered at, seeing that Mr. John Short had taken them over with the other fixtures of the office.

CHAPTER XVI.
SHORT ON LEGAL ETIQUETTE.

"Well, Meeson, what is it? Have you come to ask me to lunch?" asked Mr. John Short. "Do you know I actually thought that you might have been a client."

"Well, by Jove, old fellow, and so I am," answered Eustace. "I have been to your brother, and he has sent me on to you, because he says that it is not the etiquette of the profession to see a client unless a solicitor is present, so he has referred me to you."

"Perfectly right, perfectly right of my brother James, Meeson. Considering how small are his opportunities of becoming cognizant with the practice of his profession, it is extraordinary how well he is acquainted with its theory. And now, what is the point?"

"Well, do you know, Short, as the point is rather a long one, and as your brother said that he should expect us at two precisely, I think that we had better take the 'bus back to the Temple, when I can tell the yarn to both of you at once."

"Very well. I do not, as a general rule, like leaving my office at this time of day, as it is apt to put clients to inconvenience, especially such of them as come from a distance. But I will make an exception for you, Meeson. William," he went on, to the counterpart of the Pump-court infant, "if anyone calls to see me, will you be so good as to tell them that I am engaged in an important conference at the chambers of Mr. Short, in Pump-court, but that I hope to be back by half-past three?"

"Yes, Sir," said William, as he shut the door behind them: "certainly, Sir." And then, having placed the musty documents upon the shelf, whence they could be fetched down without difficulty on the slightest sign of a client, that ingenious youth, with singular confidence that nobody would be inconvenienced thereby, put a notice on the door to the effect that he would be back immediately, and adjourned to indulge in the passionately exhilarating game of "chuck farthing" with various other small clerks of his acquaintance.

In due course, Eustace and his legal adviser arrived at Pump-court, and, oh! how the heart of James, the barrister, swelled with pride when, for the first time in his career, he saw a real solicitor enter his chambers accompanied by a real client. He would, indeed, have preferred it if the solicitor had not happened to be his twin-brother, and the client had been some other than his intimate friend; but still it was a blessed sight—a very blessed sight!

"Will you be seated, gentlemen?" he said with much dignity.

They obeyed.

"And now, Meeson, I suppose that you have explained to my brother the matter on which you require my advice?"

"No, I haven't," said Eustace; "I thought I might as well explain it to you both together, eh?"

"Hum," said James; "it is not quite regular. According to the etiquette of the profession to which I have the honour to belong, it is not customary that matters should be so dealt with. It is usual that papers should be presented; but that I will overlook, as the point appears to be pressing."

"That's right," said Eustace. "Well, I have come to see about a will."

"So I understand," said James; "but what will, and where is it?"

"Well, it's a will in my favour, and is tattooed upon a lady's neck."

The twins simultaneously rose from their chairs, and looked at Eustace with such a ridiculous identity of movement and expression that he fairly burst out laughing.

"I presume, Meeson, that this is not a hoax," said James, severely. "I presume that you know too well what is due to learned counsel to attempt to make one of their body the victim of a practical joke?"

"Surely, Meeson," added John, "you have sufficient respect for the dignity of the law not to tamper with it in any such way as my brother has indicated?"

"Oh, certainly not. I assure you it is all square. It is a true bill, or rather a true will."

"Proceed," said James, resuming his seat. "This is evidently a case of an unusual nature."

"You are right there, old boy," said Eustace. "And now, just listen," and he proceeded to unfold his moving tale with much point and emphasis.

When he had finished John looked at James rather helplessly. The case was beyond him. But James was equal to the occasion. He had mastered that first great axiom which every young barrister should lay to heart—"Never appear to be ignorant."

"This case," he said, as though he were giving judgment, "is, doubtless, of a remarkable nature, and I cannot at the moment lay my hand upon any authority bearing on the point—if, indeed, any such are to be found. But I speak off-hand, and must not be held too closely to the *obiter dictum* of a *viva voce* opinion. It seems to me that, notwithstanding its peculiar idiosyncrasies, and the various 'cruces' that it presents, it will, upon closer examination, be found to fall within those general laws that govern the legal course of testamentary disposition. If I remember aright—I speak off-hand—the Act of 1. Vic., cap. 26, specifies that a will shall be in writing, and tattooing may fairly be defined as a rude variety of writing. It is, I admit, usual that writing should be done on paper or parchment, but I have no doubt that the young lady's skin, if carefully removed and dried, would make excellent parchment. At present, therefore, it is parchment in its green stage, and perfectly available for writing purposes.

"To continue. It appears—I am taking Mr. Meeson's statement as being perfectly accurate—that the will was properly and duly executed by the testator, or rather by the person who tattooed in his presence and at his command: a form of signature which is very well covered by the section of the Act of 1. Vic., cap. 26. It seems, too, that the witnesses attested in the presence of each other and of the testator. It is true that there was no attestation clause: but the supposed necessity for an attestation clause is one of those fallacies of the lay mind which, perhaps, cluster more frequently and with a greater persistence round questions connected with testamentary disposition than those of any other branch of the law. Therefore, we must take the will to have been properly executed in accordance with the spirit of the statute.

"And now we come to what at present strikes me as the crux. The will is undated. Does that invalidate it? I answer with confidence, no. And mark: evidence—that of Lady Holmhurst—can be produced that this will did not exist upon Miss Augusta Smithers previous to Dec. 19, on which day the Kangaroo sank; and evidence can also be produced—that of Mrs. Thomas—that it did exist on Christmas Day, when Miss Smithers was rescued. It is, therefore, clear that it must have got upon her back between Dec. 19 and Dec. 25."

"Quite so, old fellow," said Eustace, much impressed at this coruscation of legal lore. "Evidently you are the man to tackle the case. But, I say, what is to be done next? You see, I'm afraid it's too late. Probate has issued, whatever that may mean."

"Probate has issued!" echoed the great James, struggling with his rising contempt; "and is the law so helpless that probate which has been allowed to issue under an erroneous apprehension of the facts cannot be recalled? Most certainly not! So soon as the preliminary formalities are concluded, a writ must be issued to revoke the probate, and claiming that the Court should pronounce in favour of the later will; or, stay, there is no executor—there is no executor!—a very important point—claiming a grant of letters of administration with the will annexed: I think that will be the better course."

"But how can you annex Miss Smithers to a 'grant of letters of administration,' whatever that may mean?" said Eustace, feebly.

"That reminds me," said James, disregarding the question and addressing his brother, "you must at once file Miss Smithers in the registry, and see to the preparation of the usual affidavit of scripts."

"Certainly, certainly," said John, as though this were the most simple business in the world.

"What?" gasped Eustace, as a vision of Augusta impaled upon an enormous bill-guard rose before his eyes. "You can't file a lady; it's impossible!"

"Impossible or not, it must be done before any further steps are taken. Let me see; I believe that Dr. Probate is the sitting Registrar at Somerset House this sittings. It would be well if you made an appointment for to-morrow."

"Yes," said John.

"Well," went on James, "I think that is all for the present. You will, of course, let me have the instructions and other papers with all possible speed. I suppose that other counsel besides myself will be ultimately retained?"

"Oh! that reminds me," said Eustace; "about money, you know. I don't quite see how I am going to pay for all this game. I have got about fifty pounds spare cash in the world, and that's all: and I know enough to be aware that fifty pounds do not go far in a lawsuit."

Blankly James looked at John and John at James. This was very trying.

"Fifty pounds will go a good way in out-of-pocket fees," suggested James, at length, rubbing his bald head with his handkerchief.

"Possibly," answered John, pettishly; "but how about the remuneration of the plaintiff's legal advisers? Can't you"—addressing Eustace—"manage to get the money from someone?"

"Well," said Eustace, "there's Lady Holmhurst. Perhaps if I offered to share the spoil with her, if there was any."

"Dear me, no," said John; "that would be 'maintenance.'"

"Certainly not," chimed in James, holding up his hand in dismay. "Most clearly it would be 'Champerty'; and did it come to the knowledge of the Court, nobody can say what might not happen."

"Indeed," answered Eustace, with a sigh, "I don't quite know what you mean, but I seem to have said something very wrong. The odds on a handicap are child's play to understand beside this law," he added sadly.

"It is obvious, James," said John, that, "putting aside other matters, this would prove, independent of pecuniary reward, a most interesting case for you to conduct."

"That is so, John," replied James; "but as you must be well aware, the etiquette of my profession will not allow me to conduct a case for nothing. Upon that point, above all others, etiquette rules us with a rod of iron. The stomach of the bar, collective and individual, is revolted and scandalised at the idea of one of its members doing anything for nothing."

"Yes," put in Eustace, "I have always understood they were regular nailers."

"Quite so, my dear James; quite so," said John, with a sweet smile. "A fee must be marked upon the brief of learned counsel, and that fee be paid to him, together with many other smaller fees; for learned counsel is like the cigarette-boxes and new-fashioned weighing-machines at the stations: he does not work unless you drop something down him. But there is nothing to prevent learned counsel from returning that fee, and all the little fees. Indeed, James, you will see that this practice is common amongst the most eminent of your profession, when, for instance, they require an advertisement or wish to pay a delicate compliment to a constituency. What do they do then? They wait till they find £500 marked upon a brief, and then resign their fee. Why should you not do the same in this case, in your own interest? Of course, if we win the cause, the other side or the estate will pay the costs; and if we lose, you will at least have had the advantage, the priceless advantage, of a unique advertisement."

"Very well, John; let it be so," said James, with magnanimity. "Your cheques for fees will be duly returned; but it must be understood that they are to be presented."

"Not at the bank," said John, hastily. "I have recently had to oblige a client," he added by way of explanation to Eustace, "and my balance is rather low."

"No," said James; "I quite understand. I was going to say 'are to be presented to my clerk.'"

And with this solemn farce, the conference came to an end.

CHAPTER XVII.
HOW AUGUSTA WAS FILED.

That very afternoon Eustace returned to Lady Holmhurst's house in Hanover-square, to tell his dear Augusta that she must attend on the following morning to be filed in the Registry at Somerset House. As may be imagined, though willing to go any reasonable length to oblige her new-found lover, Augusta not unnaturally resisted this course violently, and was supported in her resistance by her friend Lady Holmhurst, who, however, presently left the room, leaving them to settle it as they liked.

"I do think that it is a little hard," said Augusta with a stamp of her foot, "that, after all that I have gone through, I should be taken off to have my unfortunate back stared at by a Doctor some one or other, and then be shut up with a lot of musty old wills in a Registry."

"Well, my dearest girl," said Eustace, "either it must be done or else the whole thing must be given up. Mr. John Short declares that it is absolutely necessary that the document should be placed in the custody of the officer of the Court."

"But how am I going to live in a cupboard, or in an iron safe with a lot of wills?" asked Augusta, feeling very cross indeed.

"I don't know, I am sure," said Eustace; "Mr. John Short says that that is a matter which the learned Doctor will have to settle. His own opinion is that the learned Doctor—confound him!—will order that you should accompany him about wherever he goes till the trial comes off; for, you see, in that way you would never be out of the custody of an officer of the Court. But," went on Eustace, gloomily, "all I can tell him, if he makes that order, is, that if he takes you about with him he will have to take me too."

"Why?" said Augusta.

"Why? Because I don't trust him—that's why. Old? oh, yes; I dare say he is old. And, besides, just think: this learned gentleman has practised for twenty years in the Divorce Court! Now, I ask you, what can you expect from a gentleman, however learned, who has practised for twenty years in the Divorce Court? I know him," went on Eustace, vindictively—"I know him. He will fall in love with you himself. Why, he would be an old duffer if he didn't."

"Really," said Augusta, bursting out laughing, "you are too ridiculous, Eustace."

"I don't know about being ridiculous, Augusta; but if you think I am going to let you be marched about by that learned Doctor without my being there to look after you, you are mistaken. Why, of course he would fall in love with you, or some of his clerks would; nobody could be near you for a couple of days without doing so."

"Do you think so?" said Augusta, looking at him very sweetly.

"Yes, I do," he answered, and thus the conversation came to an end and was not resumed till dinner-time.

On the following morning at eleven o'clock, Eustace, who had managed to get a few days' leave from his employers, arrived with Mr. John Short to take Augusta and Lady Holmhurst—who was going to chaperon her—to Somerset House, whither, notwithstanding her objections of the previous day, she had at last consented to go. Mr. Short was introduced, and much impressed both the ladies by the extraordinary air of learning and command which was stamped upon his countenance. He wanted to inspect the will at once; but Augusta struck at this, saying that it would be quite enough to have her shoulders stared at once that day. With a sigh and a shake of the head at her unreasonableness, Mr. John Short submitted, and then the carriage came round and they were all driven off to Somerset House. Presently they were there, and after threading innumerable chilly passages, reached a dismal room with an almanack, a dirty deal table, and a few chairs in it, wherein were congregated several solicitors' clerks, waiting their turn to appear before the Registrar. Here they waited for half-an-hour or more, to Augusta's considerable discomfort, for she soon found that she was an object of curiosity and closest attention to the solicitors' clerks, who never took their eyes off her. Presently she discovered the reason, for having remarkably quick ears, she overheard one of the solicitors' clerks, a callow little man with yellow hair and an enormous diamond pin, whose appearance somehow reminded her of a new-born chicken, tell another, who was evidently of the Jewish faith, that she (Augusta) was the respondent in the famous divorce case of Jones *v.* Jones, and was going to appear before the Registrar to submit herself to cross examination in some matter connected with a grant of alimony. Now, as all London was talking about the alleged iniquities of the Mrs. Jones in question, whose moral turpitude was only equalled by her beauty, Augusta did not feel best pleased, although she perceived that she instantly became an object of heartfelt admiration to the clerks.

Presently, however, somebody poked his head through the door, which he opened just wide enough to admit it, and bawling out—

"Short, re Meeson," vanished as abruptly as he had come.

"Now, Lady Holmhurst, if you please," said Mr. John Short, "allow me to show the way, if you will kindly follow with the will—this way, please."

In another minute, the unfortunate "will" found herself in a large and lofty room, at the top of which, with his back to the light, sat a most agreeable-looking middle-aged gentleman, who, as they advanced, rose with a politeness that one does not generally expect from officials on a fixed salary, and, bowing, asked them to be seated.

"Well, what can I do for you? Mr.—ah! Mr."—and he put on his eye-glasses and referred to his notes—"Mr. Short—you wish to file a will, I understand; and there are peculiar circumstances of some sort in the case?"

"Yes, Sir; there are," said Mr. John Short, with much meaning. "The will to be filed in the Registry is the last true will of Jonathan Meeson, of Pompadour Hall, in the county of Warwick, and the property concerned amounts to about two millions. Upon last motion day, the death of Jonathan Meeson, who was supposed to have sunk in the Kangaroo, was allowed to be presumed, and probate has been taken out. As a matter of fact, however, the said Jonathan Meeson perished in Kerguelen Land some days after the shipwreck, and before he died he duly executed a fresh will in favour of his nephew, Eustace H. Meeson, the gentleman before you. Miss Augusta Smithers"—

"What," said the learned Registrar, "is this Miss Smithers whom we have been reading so much about lately—the Kerguelen Land heroine?"

"Yes; I am Miss Smithers," she said with a little blush; "and this is Lady Holmhurst, whose husband"—and she checked herself.

"It gives me much pleasure to make your acquaintance, Miss Smithers," said the learned Doctor, courteously shaking hands, and bowing to Lady Holmhurst—proceedings which Eustace watched with the jaundiced eye of suspicion. "He's beginning already," said that ardent lover to himself. "I knew how it would be. Trust my Gus into his custody?—never! I had rather be committed for contempt."

"The best thing that I can do, Sir," went on John Short, impatiently, for, to his severe eye, these interruptions were not seemly, "will be to at once offer you inspection of the document, which, I may state, is of an unusual character," and he looked at Augusta, who, poor girl, coloured to the eyes.

"Quite so, quite so," said the learned Registrar. "Well, has Miss Smithers got the will? Perhaps she will produce it."

"Miss Smithers *is* the will," said Mr. John Short.

"Oh—I am afraid that I do not quite understand"—

"To be more precise, Sir, the will is tattooed on Miss Smithers."

"*What?*" almost shouted the learned Doctor, literally bounding from his chair.

"The will is tattooed upon Miss Smithers's back," continued Mr. John Short, in a perfectly unmoved tone; "and it is now my duty to offer you inspection of the document, and to take your instructions as to how you propose to file it in the Registry"—

"Inspection of the document—inspection of the document?" gasped the astonished Doctor; "How am I to inspect the document?"

"I must leave that to you, Sir," said Mr. John Short, regarding the learned Registrar's shrinking form with contempt not unmixed with pity. "The will is on the lady's back, and I, on behalf of the plaintiff, mean to get a grant with the document annexed."

Lady Holmhurst began to laugh; and as for the learned Doctor, anything more absurd than he looked, intrenched as he was behind his office chair, with perplexity written on his face, it would be impossible to imagine.

"Well," he said at length, "I suppose that I must come to a decision. It is a painful matter, very, to a person of modest temperament. However, I cannot shrink from my duty, and must face it. Therefore," he went on with an air of judicial sternness, "therefore, Miss Smithers, I must trouble you to show me this alleged will. There is a cupboard there," and he pointed to the corner of the room, "where you can make—'um—make the necessary preparations."

"Oh, it isn't quite so bad as that," said Augusta, with a sigh, and she began to remove her jacket.

"Dear me!" he said, observing her movement with alarm, "I suppose she is hardened," he continued to himself: "but I dare say one gets used to this sort of thing upon desert islands."

Meanwhile poor Augusta had got her jacket off. She was dressed in an evening dress, and had a white silk scarf over her shoulder: this she removed.

"Oh," he said, "I see—in evening dress. Well, of course, that is quite a different matter. And so that is the will—well, I have had some experience, but I never saw or heard of anything like it before. Signed and attested, but not dated. Ah! unless," he added, "the date is lower down."

"No," said Augusta, "there is no date; I could not stand any more tattooing. It was all done at one sitting, and I got faint."

"I don't wonder at it, I am sure. I think it is the bravest thing I ever heard of," and he bowed with much grace.

"Ah," muttered Eustace, "he's beginning to pay compliments now, insidious old hypocrite!"

"Well," went on the innocent and eminently respectable object of his suspicions, "of course the absence of a date does not invalidate a will—it is matter for proof, that is all. But there, I am not in a position to give any opinion about the case; it is quite beyond me, and besides, that is not my business. But now, Miss Smithers, as you have once put yourself in the custody of the Registry in the capacity of a will, might I ask if you have any suggestion to make as to how you are to be dealt with. Obviously you cannot be locked up with the other wills, and equally obviously it is against the rules to allow a will to go out of the custody of the Court, unless by special permission of the Court. Also it is clear that I cannot put any restraint upon the liberty of the subject and order you to remain with me. Indeed, I doubt if it would be possible to do so by any means short of an Act of Parliament. Under these circumstances I am, I confess, a little confused as to what course should be taken with reference to this important alleged will."

"What I have to suggest, Sir," said Mr. Short, "is that a certified copy of the will should be filed, and that there should be a special paragraph inserted in the affidavit of scripts detailing the circumstances."

"Ah," said the learned Doctor, polishing his eye-glasses, "you have given me an idea. With Miss Smithers' consent we will file something better than a certified copy of the will—we will file a photographic copy. The inconvenience to Miss Smithers will be trifling, and it may prevent questions being raised hereafter."

"Have you any objections to that, my dear?" asked Lady Holmhurst.

"Oh, no, I suppose not," said Augusta mournfully; "I seem to be public property now."

"Very well, then; excuse me for a moment," said the learned Doctor. "There is a photographer close by whom I have had occasion to employ officially. I will write and see if he can come round."

In a few minutes an answer came back from the photographer that he would be happy to wait upon Doctor Probate at three o'clock, up to which hour he was engaged.

"Well," said the Doctor, "it is clear that I cannot let Miss Smithers out of the custody of the Court till the photograph is taken. Let me see, I think that yours was my last appointment this morning. Now, what do you say to the idea of something to eat? We are not five minutes drive from Simpson's, and I shall feel delighted if you will make a pleasure of a necessity."

Lady Holmhurst, who was getting very hungry, said that she should be most pleased, and, accordingly, they all—with the exception of Mr. John Short, who departed about some business, saying that he would return at three o'clock—drove off in Lady Holmhurst's carriage to the restaurant, where this delightful specimen of the genus Registrar stood them a most sumptuous champagne lunch, and made himself so agreeable, that both the ladies nearly fell in love with him, and even Eustace was constrained to admit to himself that good things can come out of the Divorce Court. Finally, the doctor wound up the proceedings, which were of a most lively order, and included an account of Augusta's adventures, with a toast.

"I hear from Lady Holmhurst," he said, "that you two young people are going to take the preliminary step—um—towards a possible future appearance in that Court with which I had for many years the honor of being connected—that is, that you are going to get married. Now, matrimony is, according to my somewhat extended experience, an undertaking of a venturesome order, though cases occasionally come under one's observation where the results have proved to be in every way satisfactory; and I must say that, if I may form an opinion from the facts as they are before me, I never knew an engagement entered into under more promising or more romantic auspices. Here the young gentleman quarrels with his uncle in taking the part of the young lady, and thereby is disinherited of vast wealth. Then the young lady, under the most terrible circumstances, takes steps of a nature that not one woman in five hundred would have done to restore to him that wealth. Whether or no those steps will ultimately prove successful I do not know, and, if I did, like Herodotus, I should prefer not to say; but whether the wealth comes or goes, it is impossible but that a sense of mutual confidence and a mutual respect and admiration—that is, if a more quiet thing, certainly, also, a more enduring thing, than mere 'love'—must and will result from them. Mr. Meeson, you are indeed a fortunate man. In Miss Smithers you are going to marry beauty, courage, and genius, and if you will allow an older man of some experience to drop the official and give you a word of advice, it is this: always try to deserve your good fortune, and remember that a man who, in his youth, finds such a woman, and is enabled by circumstances to marry her, is indeed—

Smiled on by Joy, and cherished of the Gods.

"And now I will end my sermon, and wish you both health and happiness and fulness of days," and he drank off his glass of champagne, and looked so pleasant and kindly that Augusta longed to kiss him on the spot, and as for Eustace, he shook hands with him warmly, and then and there a friendship began between the two which endures till now.

And then they all went back to the office, and there was the photographer waiting with all his apparatus, and astonished enough he was when he found out what the job was that he had to do. However, the task proved an easy one enough, as the light of the room was suitable, and the dark lines of cuttle ink upon Augusta's neck would, the man said, come out perfectly in the photograph. So he took two or three shots at her back and then departed, saying that he would bring a life-sized reproduction to be filed in the Registry in a couple of days.

And after that the learned Registrar also shook hands with them, and said that he need detain them no longer, as he now felt justified in allowing Augusta out of his Custody.

And so they departed, glad to have got over the first step so pleasantly.

CHAPTER XVIII.
AUGUSTA FLIES.

Of course, Augusta's story, so far as it was publicly known, had created no small stir, which was considerably emphasised when pictures of her appeared in the illustrated papers, and it was discovered that she was young and charming. But the excitement, great as it was, was as nothing compared to that which arose when the first whispers of the tale of the will, which was tattooed upon her shoulders, began to get about. Paragraphs and stories about this will appeared in the papers, but of course she took no notice of these.

On the fourth day, however, after she had been photographed for the purposes of the Registry, things came to a climax. It so happened that on that morning Lady Holmhurst asked Augusta to go to a certain shop in Regent-street to get some lace which she required to trim her widow's dresses, and accordingly at about half-past twelve o'clock she started, accompanied by the lady's maid. As soon as they shut the front door of the house in Hanover-square she noticed two or three doubtful-looking men who were loitering about, and who instantly followed them, staring at her with all their eyes. She made her way along, however, without taking any notice until she got to Regent-street, by which time there were quite a score of people walking after her whispering excitedly at each other. In Regent-street itself, the first thing that she saw was a man selling photographs. Evidently he was doing a roaring trade, for there was a considerable crowd round him, and he was shouting something which she could not catch. Presently a gentleman, who had bought one of the photographs, stopped just in front of her to look at it, and as he was short and Augusta was tall, she could see over his shoulder, and the next second started back with an indignant exclamation. "No wonder!" for the photograph was one of herself as she had been taken in the low dress in the Registry. There was no mistake about it—there was the picture of the will tattooed right across her shoulders.

Nor did her troubles end there, for at that moment a man came bawling down the street carrying a number of the first edition of an evening paper—

"Description and picture of the lovely 'eroine of the Cockatoo," he yelled, "with the will tattooed upon 'er! Taken from the original photograph! Facsimile picture!"

"Oh, dear me," said Augusta to the maid, "that is really too bad. Let us go home."

But meanwhile the crowd at her back had gathered and increased to an extraordinary extent and was slowly inclosing her in a circle. The fact was, that the man who had followed her from Hanover-square had told the others who joined their ranks, who the lady was, and she was now identified.

"That's her," said one man.

"Who?" said another.

"Why, the Miss Smithers as escaped from the Kangaroo and has the will on her back, in course."

There was a howl of exultation from the mob, and in another second the wretched Augusta was pressed, together with the lady's maid, who began to scream with fright, right up against a lamp-post, while a crowd of eager faces, mostly unwashed, were pushed almost into her own. Indeed, so fierce was the crowd in its attempt to get a glimpse of the latest curiosity, that she began to think that she would be thrown down and trampled under foot, when timely relief arrived in the shape of two policemen and a gentleman volunteer, who managed to rescue her and get them into a hansom cab, which started for Hanover-square, pursued by a shouting crowd of nondescript individuals.

Now, Augusta was a woman of good nerve and resolution; but this sort of thing was too trying, and, accordingly, accompanied by Lady Holmhurst, she went off, that very day, to some rooms in a little riverside hotel on the Thames.

When Eustace, walking down the Strand that afternoon, found every photograph-shop full of accurate pictures of the shoulders of his beloved, he was simply furious; and, rushing to the photographer who had taken the picture in the Registry, threatened him with proceedings of every sort and kind. The man admitted outright that he had put the photographs upon the market, saying that he had never stipulated not to do so, and that he could not afford to throw away five or six hundred pounds when a chance of making it came in his way.

Thereon Eustace departed, still vowing vengeance, to consult the legal twins. As a result of this, within a week, Mr. James Short made a motion for and injunction against the photographer, restraining the sale of the photographs in question, on the ground that such sale, being of copies of a document vital to a cause now pending in the Court, those copies having been obtained through the instrumentality of an officer of the court, Dr. Probate, the sale thereof amounted to a contempt, inasmuch as, if for no other reason, the photographer who obtained them became technically, and for that purpose only, an officer of the Court, and had, therefore, no right to part with them, or any of them, without the leave of the Court. It will be remembered that this motion gave rise to some very delicate questions connected with the powers of the Court in such a matter, and also incidentally with the law of photographic copyright. It is also memorable for the unanimous and luminous judgment finally delivered by the Lords Justices of Appeal, whereby the sale of the photographs was stopped, and the photographer was held to have been guilty of a technical contempt. This judgment contained perhaps the most searching and learned definition of constructive contempt that has yet been formulated: but for the text of this, I must refer the student to the law reports, because, as it took two hours to deliver, I fear that it would, notwithstanding its many beauties, be thought too long for the purpose of this history. Unfortunately, however, it did not greatly benefit Augusta, the victim of the unlawful dissemination of photographs of her shoulders, inasmuch as the judgment was not delivered till a week after the great case of Meeson *v.* Addison and Another had been settled.

About a week after Augusta's adventure in Regent-street, a motion was made in the Court of Probate on behalf of the defendants, Messrs. Addison and Roscoe, who were the executors and principal beneficiaries under the former will of November, 1885, demanding that the Court should order the plaintiff to file a further and better affidavit of scripts, with the original will got up by him attached, the object, of course, being to compel an inspection of the document. This motion, which first brought the whole case under the notice of the public, was strenuously resisted by Mr. James Short, and resulted in the matter being referred to the learned Registrar for his report. On the next motion day this report was presented, and, on its appearing from it that the photography had taken place in his presence and accurately represented the tattoo marks on the lady's shoulders, the Court declined to harass the "will" by ordering her to submit to any further inspection before the trial. It was on this occasion that it transpired that the will was engaged to be married to the plaintiff, a fact at which the Court metaphorically opened its eyes. After this the defendants obtained leave to amend their answer to the plaintiff's statement of claim. At first they had only pleaded that the testator had not duly executed the alleged will in accordance with the provisions of 1 Vic., cap. 26, sec. 2, and that he did not know and approve the contents thereof. But now they added a plea to the effect that the said alleged will was obtained by the undue influence of Augusta Smithers, or, as one of the learned counsel for the defendants put it much more clearly at the trial, "that the will had herself procured the will, by an undue projection of her own will upon the unwilling mind of the testator."

And so the time went on. As often as he could, Eustace got away from London, and went down to the little riverside hotel, and was as happy as a man can be who has a tremendous law suit hanging over him. The law, no doubt, is an admirable institution, out of which a large number of people make a living, and a proportion of benefit accrues to the community at large. But woe unto those who form the subject-matter of its operations. For instance, the Court of Chancery is an excellent institution in theory, and looks after the affairs of minors upon the purest principles. But how many of its wards after, and as a result of one of its well-intentioned interferences, have to struggle for the rest of their lives under a load of debt raised to pay the crushing costs! To employ the Court of Chancery to look after wards is something as though one set a tame elephant to pick up pins. No doubt he could pick them up, but it would cost something to feed him. It is a perfectly arguable proposition that the Court of Chancery produces as much wretchedness and poverty as it prevents, and it certainly is a bold step, except under the most exceptionable circumstances, to place anybody in its custody who has money that can be dissipated in law expenses. But of course these are revolutionary remarks, which one cannot expect everybody to agree with, least of all the conveyancing counsel of the Court.

However this may be, certainly his impending lawsuit proved a fly in Eustace's honey. Never a day passed but some fresh worry arose. James and John, the legal twins, fought like heroes, and held their own although their experience was so small—as men of talent almost invariably do when they are put to it. But it was difficult for Eustace to keep them supplied even with sufficient money for out-of-pocket expenses; and, of course, as was natural in a case in which such enormous sums were at stake, and in which the defendants were already men of vast wealth, they found the flower of the entire talent and weight of the Bar arrayed against them. Naturally Eustace felt, and so did Mr. James Short—who, notwithstanding his pomposity and the technicality of his talk, was both a clever and sensible man—that more counsel, men of weight and experience, ought to be briefed; but there were absolutely no funds for this purpose, nor was anybody likely to advance any upon the security of a will tattooed upon a young lady's back. This was awkward, because success in law proceedings so very often leans towards the weightiest purse, and Judges however impartial, being but men after all, are more apt to listen to an argument which is urged upon their attention by an Attorney-General than on one advanced by an unknown junior.

However, there the fact was, and they had to make the best of it; and a point in their favour was that the case, although of a most remarkable nature, was comparatively simple, and did not involve any great mass of documentary evidence.

CHAPTER XIX.
MEESON *v.* ADDISON AND ANOTHER.

The most wearisome times go by at last if only one lives to see the end of them, and so it came to pass that at length on one fine morning about a quarter to ten of the Law Courts' clock, that projects its ghastly hideousness upon unoffending Fleet-street, Augusta, accompanied by Eustace, Lady Holmhurst, and Mrs. Thomas, the wife of Captain Thomas, who had come up from visiting her relatives in the Eastern counties in order to give evidence, found herself standing in the big entrance to the new Law Courts, feeling as though she would give five years of her life to be anywhere else.

"This way, my dear," said Eustace; "Mr. John Short said that he would meet us by the statue in the hall." Accordingly they passed into the archway by the oak stand where the cause-lists are displayed. Augusta glanced at them as she went, and the first thing that her eyes fell on was "Probate and Divorce Division Court I., at 10.30, Meeson *v.* Addison and Another," and the sight made her feel ill. In another moment they had passed a policeman of gigantic size, "monstrum horrendum, informe, ingens," who watches and wards the folding-doors through which so much human learning, wretchedness, and worry pass day by day, and were standing in the long, but narrow and ill-proportioned hall which appears to have been the best thing that the architectural talent of the nineteenth century was capable of producing.

To the right of the door on entering is a statue of the architect of a pile of which England has certainly no cause to feel proud, and here, a black bag full of papers in his hand, stood Mr. John Short, wearing that air of excitement upon his countenance which is so commonly to be seen in the law courts.

"Here you are," he said, "I was beginning to be afraid that you would be late. We are first on the list, you know; the judge fixed it specially to suit the convenience of the Attorney-General. He's on the other side, you know," he added, with a sigh. "I'm sure I don't know how poor James will get on. There are more than twenty counsel against him, for all the legatees under the former will are represented. At any rate, he is well up in his facts, and there does not seem to me to be very much law in the case."

Meanwhile, they had been proceeding up the long hall till they came to a poky little staircase which had just been dug out in the wall, the necessity for a staircase at that end of the hall, whereby the court floor could be reached having, to all appearance, originally escaped the attention of the architect. On getting to the top of the staircase they turned to the left and then to the left again. If they had had any doubt as to which road they should take it would have been speedily decided by the long string of wigs which were streaming away in the direction of Divorce Court No. 1. Thicker and thicker grew the wigs; it was obvious that the *cause célèbre* of Meeson *v.* Addison and Another would not want for hearers. Indeed, Augusta and her friends soon realised the intensity of the public interest in a way that was as impressive as it was disagreeable, for just past the Admiralty Court the passage was entirely blocked by an enormous mass of barristers; there might have been five hundred or more of them. There they were, choked up together in their white-wigged ranks, waiting for the door of the court to be opened. At present it was guarded by six or eight attendants, who, with the help of a wooden barrier, attempted to keep the surging multitude at bay—while those behind cried, "Forward!" and those in front cried "Back!"

"How on earth are we going to get through?" asked Augusta, and at that moment Mr. John Short caught hold of an attendant who was struggling about in the skirts of the crowd like a fly in a cup of tea, and asked him the same question, explaining that their presence was necessary to the show.

"I'm bothered if I know, Sir; you can't come this way. I suppose I must let you through by the underground passage from the other court. Why," he went on, as he led the way to the Admiralty Court, "hang me, if I don't believe that we shall all be crushed to death by them there barristers: It would take a regiment of cavalry to keep them back. And they are a 'ungry lot, they are; and they ain't no work to do, and that's why they comes kicking and tearing and worriting just to see a bit of painting on a young lady's shoulders."

By this time they had passed through the Admiralty Court, which was not sitting, and been conducted down a sort of well, that terminated in the space occupied by the Judge's clerks and other officers of the Court. In another minute they found themselves emerging in a similar space in the other court.

Before taking the seat that was pointed out to her and the other witnesses in the well of the court, immediately below those reserved for Queen's counsel, Augusta glanced round. The body of the court was as yet quite empty, for the seething mob outside had not yet burst in, though their repeated shouts of "Open the door!" could be plainly heard. But the jury box was full, not with a jury, for the case was to be tried before the Court itself, but of various distinguished individuals, including several ladies, who had obtained orders. The little gallery above was also crowded with smart-looking people. As for the seats devoted to counsel in the cause, they were crammed to overflowing with the representatives of the various defendants—so crammed, indeed, that the wretched James Short, sole counsel for the plaintiff, had to establish himself and his papers in the centre of the third bench sometimes used by solicitors.

"Heavens!" said Eustace to Augusta, counting the heads; "there are twenty-three counsel against us. What will that unfortunate James do against so many?"

"I don't know, I'm sure," said Augusta, with a sigh. "It doesn't seem quite fair, does it? But then, you see, there was no money."

Just then John Short came up. He had been to speak to his brother. Augusta being a novelist, and therefore a professional student of human physiognomy, was engaged in studying the legal types before her, which she found resolved themselves into two classes—the sharp, keen-faced class and the solid, heavy-jawed class.

"Who on earth are they all?" she asked.

"Oh," he said, "that's the Attorney-General. He appears with Fiddlestick, Q.C., Pearl, and Bean for the defendant Addison. Next to him is the Solicitor-General, who, with Playford, Q.C., Middlestone, Blowhard, and Ross, is for the other defendant, Roscoe. Next to him is Turphy, Q.C., with the spectacles on; he is supposed to have a great effect on a jury. I don't know the name of his junior, but he looks as though he were going to eat one—doesn't he? He is for one of the legatees. That man behind is Stickon; he is for one of the legatees also. I suppose that he finds probate and divorce an interesting subject, because he is always writing books about them. Next to him is Howles, who, my brother says, is the best comic actor in the court. The short gentleman in the middle is Telly; he reports for the *Times*. You see, as this is an important case, he has got somebody to help him to take it—that long man with a big wig. He, by-the-way, writes novels, like you do, only not half such good ones. The next"—but at this moment Mr. John Short was interrupted by the approach of a rather good-looking man, who wore an eye-glass continually fixed in his right eye. He was Mr. News, of the great firm News and News, who were conducting the case on behalf of the defendants.

"Mr. Short, I believe?" said Mr. News, contemplating his opponent's youthful form with pity, not unmixed with compassion.

"Yes."

"Um, Mr. Short, I have been consulting with my clients and—um, the Attorney and Solicitor-General and Mr. Fiddlestick, and we are quite willing to admit that there are circumstances of doubt in this case which would justify us in making an offer of settlement."

"Before I can enter into that, Mr. News," said John, with great dignity, "I must request the presence of my counsel."

"Oh, certainly," said Mr. News, and accordingly James was summoned from his elevated perch, where he was once more going through his notes and the heads of his opening speech, although he already knew his brief—which, to do it justice, had been prepared with extraordinary care and elaboration—almost by heart, and next moment, for the first time in his life, found himself in consultation with an Attorney and a Solicitor-General.

"Look here, Short," said the first of these great men addressing James as though he had known him intimately for years, though, as a matter of fact, he had only that moment ascertained his name from Mr. Fiddlestick, who was himself obliged to refer to Bean before he could be sure of it—"look here, Short: don't you think that we can settle this business? You've got a strongish case; but there are some ugly things against you, as no doubt you know."

"I don't quite admit that," said James.

"Of course—of course," said Mr. Attorney; "but still, in my judgment, if you will not be offended at my expressing it, you are not quite on firm ground. Supposing, for instance, your young lady is not allowed to give evidence?"

"I think," said a stout gentleman behind who wore upon his countenance the very sweetest and most infantile smile that Eustace had ever seen, breaking in rather hastily, as though he was afraid that his learned leader was showing too much of his hand, "I think that the case is one that, looked at from either point of view, will bear settlement better than fighting—eh, Fiddlestick? But then, I'm a man of peace," and again he smiled most seductively at James.

"What are your terms?" asked James.

The eminent counsel on the front bench turned round and stuck their wigs together like a lot of white-headed crows over a bone, and the slightly less eminent but still highly distinguished juniors on the second bench craned forward to listen.

"They are going to settle it," Eustace heard the barrister who was reporting for the *Times* say to his long assistant.

"They always do settle every case of public interest," grunted the long man in answer; "we shan't see Miss Smithers' shoulders now. Well, I shall get an introduction to her, and ask her to show them to me. I take a great interest in tattooing."

Meanwhile, Fiddlestick, Q.C., had been writing something on a strip of paper and handed to his leader, the Attorney-General (who, Mr. James Short saw with respectful admiration, had 500 guineas marked upon his brief). He nodded carelessly, and passed it on to his junior, who gave it in turn to the

Solicitor-General and Playford, Q.C. When it had gone the rounds, Mr. News took it and showed it to his two privileged clients, Messrs. Addison and Roscoe. Addison was a choleric-looking, fat-faced man. Roscoe was sallow, and had a thin, straggly black beard. When they looked at it, Addison groaned fiercely as a wounded bull, and Roscoe sighed, and that sigh and groan told Augusta—who, womanlike, had all her wits about her, and was watching every act of the drama—more than it was meant to do. It told her that these gentlemen were doing something that they did not like, and doing it because they evidently believed that they had no other course open to them. Then Mr. News gave the paper to Mr. John Short, who glanced at it and handed it on to his brother, and Eustace read it over his shoulder. It was very short, and ran thus:—"Terms offered: Half the property, and defendants pay all costs."

"Well, Short," said Eustace, "what do you say, shall we take it?"

James removed his wig, and thoughtfully rubbed his bald head. "It is a very difficult position to be put in," he said. "Of course a million is a large sum of money; but there are two at stake. My own view is that we had better fight the case out; though, of course, this is a certainty, and the result of the case is not."

"I am inclined to settle," said Eustace; "not because of the case, for I believe in it, but because of Augusta—of Miss Smithers: you see she will have to show the tattooing again, and that sort of thing is very unpleasant for a lady."

"Oh, as to that," said James loftily, "at present she must remember that she is not a lady, but a legal document. However, let us ask her."

"Now, Augusta, what shall we do?" said Eustace, when he had explained the offer; "you see, if we take the offer you will be spared a very disagreeable time. You must make up your mind quick, for the Judge will be here in a minute."

"Oh, never mind me," said Augusta, quickly; "I am used to disagreeables. No, I shall fight, I tell you they are afraid of you. I can see it in the face of that horrid Mr. Addison. Just now he positively glared at me and ground his teeth, and he would not do that if he thought that he was going to win. No, dear; I shall fight it out now."

"Very well," said Eustace, and he took a pencil and wrote, "Declined with thanks," at the foot of the offer.

Just at that moment there came a dull roar from the passage beyond. The doors of the court were being opened. Another second, and in rushed and struggled a hideous sea of barristers. Heavens, how they fought and kicked! A maddened herd of buffaloes could not have behaved more desperately.

On rushed the white wave of wigs, bearing the strong men who held the door before them like wreckage on a breaker. On they came and in forty seconds the court was crowded to its utmost capacity, and still there were hundreds of white wigged men behind. It was a fearful scene.

"Good gracious!" thought Augusta to herself, "how on earth do they all get a living?" a question that many of them would have found it hard enough to answer.

Then suddenly an old gentleman near her, whom she discovered to be the usher, jumped up and called "Silence!" in commanding accents, without producing much effect, however, on the palpitating mass of humanity in front. Then in came the officers of the Court; and a moment afterwards, everybody rose as the Judge entered, and, looking, as Augusta thought, very cross when he saw the crowded condition of the court, bowed to the bar and took his seat.

CHAPTER XX.
JAMES BREAKS DOWN.

The Registrar, not Augusta's dear doctor Probate, but another Registrar, rose and called on the case of Meeson *v.* Addison and Another, and in an instant the wretched James Short was on his legs to open the case.

"What is that gentleman's name?" Augusta heard the Judge ask of the clerk, after making two or three frantic efforts to attract his attention—a proceeding that the position of his desk rendered very difficult.

"Short, my Lord."

"Do you appear alone for the plaintiff, Mr. Short?" asked the Judge, with emphasis.

"Yes, my Lord, I do," answered James, and as he said it every pair of eyes in that crowded assembly fixed themselves upon him, and a sort of audible smile seemed to run round the court. The thing not unnaturally struck the professional mind as ludicrous and without precedent.

"And who appears for the defendant?"

"I understand, my Lord," said the learned Attorney-General, "that all my learned friends on these two benches appear together, with myself, for one or other of the defendants, or are watching the case in the interest of legatees."

Here a decided titter interrupted him.

"I may add that the interests involved in this case are very large indeed, which accounts for the number of counsel connected in one way or other with the defence."

"Quite so, Mr. Attorney," said the Judge: "but, really, the forces seem a little out of proportion. Of course the matter is not one in which the Court can interfere."

"If your Lordship will allow me," said James, "the only reason that the plaintiff is so poorly represented is that the funds to brief other counsel were, I understand, not forthcoming. I am, however, well versed in the case and, with your Lordship's permission, will do my best with it."

"Very well, Mr. Short," said the learned Judge, looking at him almost with pity, "state your case."

James—in the midst of a silence that could be felt—unfolded his pleadings, and, as he did so, for the first time a sickening sense of nervousness took hold of him and made him tremble, and, of a sudden, his mind became dark.

Most of us have undergone this sensation at one time or another, with less cause then had poor James. There he was, put up almost for the first time in his life to conduct, single-handed, a most important case, upon which it was scarcely too much to say the interest of the entire country was concentrated. Nor was this all. Opposed to him were about twenty counsel, all of them men of experience, and including in their ranks some of the most famous leaders in England: and, what was more, the court was densely crowded with scores of men of his own profession, every one of whom was, he felt, regarding him with curiosity not unmixed with pity. Then, there was the tremendous responsibility which literally seemed to crush him, though he had never quite realised it before.

"May it please your Lordship," he began; and then, as I have said, his mind became a ghastly blank, in which dim and formless ideas flitted vaguely to and fro.

There was a pause—a painful pause.

"Read your pleadings aloud," whispered a barrister who was sitting next him, and realised his plight.

This was an idea. One can read pleadings when one cannot collect one's ideas to speak. It is not usual to do so. The counsel in a cause states the substance of the pleadings, leaving the Court to refer to them if it thinks necessary. But still there was nothing absolutely wrong about it; so he snatched at the papers and promptly began:

"(I.) The plaintiff is the sole and universal legatee under the true last will of Jonathan Meeson, deceased, late of Pompadour Hall, in the County of Warwick, who died on the 23rd of December, 1885, the said will being undated, but duly executed on, or subsequent to, the 22nd day of December, 1885."

Here the learned Judge lifted his eyebrows in remonstrance, and cleared his throat preparatory to interfering; but apparently thought better of it, for he took up a blue pencil and made a note of the date of the will.

"(II.)," went on James. "On the 21st day of May, 1886, probate of an alleged will of the said Jonathan Meeson was granted to the defendants, the said will bearing date the 10th day of November, 1885. The plaintiff claims—

"(1.) That the court shall revoke probate of the said alleged will of the said Jonathan Meeson, bearing date the 10th day of November, 1885, granted to the defendants on the 21st day of May, 1886.

"(2.) A grant of letters of administration to the plaintiff with the will executed on or subsequent to the 22nd day of December,1885, annexed. (Signed) JAMES SHORT."

"May it please your Lordship," James began, again feeling dimly that he had read enough pleadings, "the defendants have filed an answer pleading that the will of the 22nd of December was not duly executed in accordance with the statute, and that the testator did not know and approve its contents, and an amended answer pleading that the said alleged will, if executed, was obtained by the undue influence of Augusta Smithers"—and once more his nervousness overcame him, and he pulled up with a jerk.

Then came another pause even more dreadful than the first.

The Judge took another note, as slowly as he could, and once more cleared his throat; but poor James could not go on. He could only wish that he might then and there expire, rather than face the hideous humiliation of such a failure. But he would have failed, for his very brain was whirling like that of a drunken man, had it not been for an occurrence that caused him for ever after to bless the name of Fiddlestick, Q.C., as the name of an eminent counsel is not often blessed in this ungrateful world. For Fiddlestick, Q.C., who, it will be remembered, was one of the leaders for the defendants, had been watching his unfortunate antagonist, till, realising how sorry was his plight, a sense of pity filled his learned breast. Perhaps he may have remembered some occasion, in the dim and distant corner of the past, when he had suffered from a similar access of frantic terror, or perhaps he may have been sorry to think that a young man should lose such an unrivalled opportunity of making a name. Anyhow, he did a noble act. As it happened, he was sitting at the right-hand corner of the Queen's counsel seats, and piled upon the desk before him was a tremendous mass of law reports which his clerk had arranged there, containing cases to which it might become necessary to refer. Now, in the presence of these law reports, Mr. Fiddlestick, in the goodness of his heart, saw an opportunity of creating a diversion, and he created it with a vengeance. For, throwing his weight suddenly forward as though by accident, or in a movement of impatience, he brought his bent arm against the pile with such force, that he sent every book, and there must have been more than twenty of them, over the desk, right on to the head and shoulders of his choleric client, Mr. Addison, who was sitting immediately beneath, on the solicitors' bench.

Down went the books with a crash and a bang, and, carried away by their weight, down went Mr. Addison on to his nose among them—a contingency that Fiddlestick, Q.C., by-the-way, had not foreseen, for he had overlooked the fact of his client's vicinity.

The Judge made an awful face, and then, realising the ludicrous nature of the scene, his features relaxed into a smile. But Mr. Addison did not smile. He bounded up off the floor, books slipping off his back in every direction, and, holding his nose (which was injured) with one hand, came skipping right at his learned adviser.

"You did it on purpose!" he almost shouted, quite forgetting where he was; "just let me get at him, I'll have his wig off!" and then, without waiting for any more, the entire audience burst out into a roar of laughter, which, however, unseemly, was perfectly reasonable; during which Mr. Fiddlestick could be seen apologising in dumb show, with a bland smile upon his countenance, while Mr. News and Mr. Roscoe between them dragged the outraged Addison to his seat, and proffered him handkerchiefs to wipe his bleeding nose.

James saw the whole thing, and forgetting his position, laughed too; and, for some mysterious reason, with the laugh his nervousness passed away.

The usher shouted "Silence!" with tremendous energy, and before the sound had died away James was addressing the Court in a clear and vigorous voice, conscious that he was a thorough master of his case, and the words to state it in would not fail him. Fiddlestick, Q.C., had saved him!

"May it please your Lordship," he began, "the details of this case are of as remarkable an order as any that to my knowledge have been brought before the Court. The plaintiff, Eustace Meeson, is the sole next-of-kin of Jonathan Meeson, Esquire, the late head of the well known Birmingham publishing firm of Meeson, Addison, and Roscoe. Under a will, bearing date the 8th of May, 1880, the plaintiff was left sole heir to the great wealth of his uncle—that is, with the exception of some legacies. Under a second will, now relied on by the defendants, and dated the 10th November, 1885, the plaintiff was entirely disinherited, and the present defendants, together with some six or eight legatees, were constituted the sole beneficiaries. On or about the 22nd December, 1885, however, the testator executed a third testamentary document under which the plaintiff takes the entire property, and this is the document now propounded. This testamentary document, or, rather, will—for I submit that it is in every sense a properly executed will—is tattooed upon the shoulders"—(Sensation in the court)—"is tattooed upon the shoulders of a young lady, Miss Augusta Smithers, who will presently be called before your Lordship; and to prevent any misunderstanding, I may as well at once state that since this event this lady has become engaged to be married to the plaintiff (Renewed sensation.)

"Such, my Lord, are the main outlines of the case that I have to present for the consideration of the Court, which I think your Lordship will understand is of so remarkable and unprecedented a nature that I must crave your Lordship's indulgence if I proceed to open it at some length, beginning the history at its commencement."

By this time James Short had completely recovered his nerve, and was, indeed, almost oblivious of the fact that there was anybody present in the court, except the learned Judge and himself. Going back to the beginning, he detailed the early history of the relationship between Eustace Meeson and his uncle, the publisher, with which this record has nothing to do. Thence he passed to the history of Augusta's relation with the firm of Meeson and Co., which, as nearly everybody in the court, not excepting the Judge, had read "Jemima's Vow," was very interesting to his auditors. Then he went on to the scene between Augusta and the publisher, and detailed how Eustace had interfered, which interference had led to a violent quarrel, resulting in the young man's disinheritance. Passing on, he detailed how the publisher and the published had taken passage in the same vessel, and the tragic occurrences which followed down to Augusta's final rescue and arrival in England, and finally ended his spirited opening by appealing to the Court not to allow its mind to be influenced by the fact that since these events the two chief actors had become engaged to be married, which struck him, he said, as a very fitting climax to so romantic a story.

At last he ceased, and amidst a little buzz of applause, for the speech had really been a very fine one, sat down. As he did so he glanced at the clock. He had been on his legs for nearly two hours, and yet it seemed to him but a very little while. In another moment he was up again and had called his first witness—Eustace Meeson.

Eustace's evidence was of a rather formal order, and was necessarily limited to an account of the relations between his uncle and himself, and between himself and Augusta. Such as it was, however, he gave it very well, and with a complete openness that appeared to produce a favorable impression on the Court.

Then Fiddlestick, Q.C., rose to cross-examine, devoting his efforts to trying to make Eustace admit that his behaviour had been of a nature to amply justify his uncle's behaviour. But there was not very much to be made out of it. Eustace detailed all that had passed freely enough, and it simply amounted to the fact that there had been angry words between the two as regards the treatment that Augusta had met with at the hands of the firm. In short, Fiddlestick could not do anything with him, and, after ten minutes of it, sat down without having advanced the case to any appreciable extent. Then several of the other counsel asked a question or two apiece, after which Eustace was told to stand down, and Lady Holmhurst was called. Lady Holmhurst's evidence was very short, merely amounting to the fact that she had seen Augusta's shoulders on board the Kangaroo, and that there was not then a sign of tattoo marks upon them, and when she saw them again in London they were tattooed. No attempt was made to cross-examine her, and on the termination of her evidence, the Court adjourned for lunch. When it reassembled James Short called Augusta, and a murmur of expectation arose from the densely crowded audience, as—feeling very sick at heart, and looking more beautiful than ever—she stepped towards the box.

As she did so the Attorney-General rose.

"I must object, my Lord," he said, "on behalf of the defendants, to this witness being allowed to enter the box."

"Upon what grounds, Mr. Attorney?" said his Lordship.

"Upon the ground that her mouth is, *ipso facto*, closed. If we are to believe the plaintiff's story, this young lady is herself the will of Jonathan Meeson, and, being so, is certainly, I submit, not competent to give evidence. There is no precedent for a document giving evidence, and I presume that the witness must be looked upon as a document."

"But, Mr. Attorney," said the Judge, "a document is evidence, and evidence of the best sort."

"Undoubtedly, my Lord; and we have no objection to the document being exhibited for the court to draw its own conclusion from, but we deny that it is entitled to speak in its own explanation. A document is a thing which speaks by its written characters. It cannot take to itself a tongue, and speak by word of mouth also; and, in support of this, I may call your Lordship's attention to the general principles of law governing the interpretation of written documents."

"I am quite aware of those principles, Mr. Attorney, and I cannot see that they touch this question."

"As your Lordship pleases. Then I will fall back upon my main contention, that Miss Smithers is, for the purposes of this case, a document and nothing but a document, and has no more right to open her mouth in support of the plaintiff's case, than would any paper will, if it could be miraculously endowed with speech."

"Well," said the Judge, "it certainly strikes me as a novel point. What have you to say to it, Mr. Short?"

All eyes were now turned upon James, for it was felt that if the point was decided against him the case was lost.

"The point to which I wish you to address yourself, Mr. Short," went on the learned Judge, "is—Is the personality of Miss Smithers so totally lost and merged in what, for want of a better term I must call her documentary capacity, as to take away from her the right to appear before this Court like any other sane human being, and give evidence of events connected with its execution?"

"If your Lordship pleases," said James, "I maintain that this is not so. I maintain that the document remains the document; and that for all purposes, including the giving of evidence concerning its execution, Miss Smithers still remains Miss Smithers. It would surely be absurd to argue that because a person has a deed executed upon her she was, *ipso facto*, incapacitated from giving evidence concerning it, on the mere ground that she was *it*. Further, such a decision would be contrary to equity and good policy, for persons could not so lightly be deprived of their natural rights. Also, in this case, the plaintiff's action would be absolutely put an end to by any such decision, seeing that the signature of Jonathan Meeson and the attesting witnesses to the will could not, of course, be recognised in their tattooed form, and there is no other living person who could depose under what circumstances the signature came to be there. I submit that the objection should be overruled."

"This," said his Lordship, in giving his decision, "is a very curious point, and one which, when first raised by the learned Attorney-General, struck me with some force; but, on considering it and hearing Mr. Short, I am convinced that it is an objection that cannot be supported" (here Eustace gave a sigh of relief). "It is argued on the part of the defendant that Miss Smithers is, for the purposes of this case a document, a document, and nothing but a document, and as such that her mouth is shut. Now, I think that the learned Attorney-General cannot have thought this matter out when he came to that conclusion. What are the circumstances? A will is supposed to have been tattooed upon this lady's skin; but is the skin the whole person? Does not the intelligence remain, and the individuality? I think that I can put what I mean more clearly by means of an illustration. Let us suppose that I were to uphold the defendant's objection, and that, as a consequence, the plaintiff's case were to break down. Then let us suppose that the plaintiff had persuaded the witness to be partially skinned"—(here Augusta nearly jumped from her seat)—"and that she, having survived the operation, was again tendered to the court as a witness, would the Court then be able, under any possibility, to refuse to accept her evidence? The document, in the form of human parchment, would then be in the hands of the officers of the Court, and the person from whom the parchment had been removed, would also be before the Court. Could it be still maintained that the two were so identical and inseparable that the disabilities attaching to a document must necessarily attach to the person? In my opinion, certainly not. Or, to take another case, let us suppose that the will had been tattooed upon the leg of a person, and, under similar circumstances, the leg were cut off and produced before the Court, either in a flesh or a mummified condition; could it then be seriously advanced that because the inscribed leg—standing on the table before the Court—had once belonged to the witness sitting in the witness-box, therefore it was not competent for the witness to give evidence on account of his or her documentary attributes? Certainly it could not.

Therefore, it seems to me that that which is separable must, for the purpose of law, be taken as already separated, and that the will on the back of this witness must be looked upon as though it were in the hands at this moment, of the officers of the Court, and consequently I overrule the objection."

"Will your Lordship take a note of your Lordship's decision?" asked the Attorney-General in view of an appeal.

"Certainly, Mr. Attorney. Let this witness be sworn."

CHAPTER XXI.
GRANT AS PRAYED.

Accordingly, Augusta was sworn, and Eustace observed that when she removed her veil to kiss the Book the sight of her sweet face produced no small effect upon the crowded court.

Then James began his examination in chief, and, following the lines which he had laid down in his opening speech, led her slowly, whilst allowing her to tell her own story as much as possible, to the time of the tattooing of the will on Kerguelen Land. All along, the history had evidently interested everybody in the court—not excepting the Judge—intensely; but now the excitement rose to boiling point.

"Well," said James, "tell his Lordship exactly how it came to pass that the will of Mr. Meeson was tattooed upon your shoulders."

In quiet but dramatic language Augusta accordingly narrated every detail, from the time when Meeson confided to her his remorse at having disinherited his nephew up to the execution of the will at her suggestion by the sailor upon her own shoulders.

"And now, Miss Smithers," said James, when she had done, "I am very sorry to have to do so; but I must ask you to exhibit the document to the Court."

Poor Augusta coloured and her eyes filled with tears, as she slowly undid the dust-cloak which hid her shoulders (for, of course, she had come in low dress). The Judge, looking up sharply, observed her natural distress.

"If you prefer it, Miss Smithers," said his Lordship, courteously, "I will order the court to be cleared of every-one except those who are actually engaged in the case."

At these ominous words a shudder of disgust passed through the densely-packed ranks. It would indeed, they felt, after all their striving, be hard if they were deprived of the sight of the will; and they stared at her despairingly, to see what she would answer.

"I thank your Lordship," she said, with a little bow; "but there would still be so many left that I do not think that it would greatly matter. I hope that everybody will understand my position, and extend their consideration to me."

"Very well," said the Judge, and without further ado she took off the cloak, and the silk handkerchief beneath it, and stood before the court dressed in a low black dress.

"I am afraid that I must ask you to come up here," said his Lordship. Accordingly she walked round, mounted the bench, and then turned her back to the Judge, in order that he might examine what was written on it. This he did very carefully with the aid of a magnifying glass, referring now and again to the photographic copy which Doctor Probate had filed in the Registry.

"Thank you," he said presently, "that will do. I am afraid that the learned counsel below will wish to have an opportunity of inspection."

So Augusta had to descend and slowly walk along the ranks, stopping before every learned leader to be carefully examined, while hundreds of eager eyes in the background were fixed upon her unfortunate neck. However, at last it came to an end.

"That will do, Miss Smithers," said the Judge, for whose consideration she felt deeply grateful; "you can put on your cloak again now." Accordingly she did so and re-entered the box.

"The document which you have just shown the Court, Miss Smithers," said James, "is the one which was executed upon you in Kerguelen Land on or about the 22nd day of December last year?"

"It is."

"It was, I understand, executed in the presence of the testator and the two attesting witnesses, all three being present together, and the signature of each being tattooed in the presence of the other?"

"It was."

"Was the testator, so far as you could judge, at the time of the dictation and execution of the will, of sound mind, memory, and understanding?"

"Most certainly he was."

"Did you, beyond the suggestions of which you have already given evidence, in any way unduly influence the testator's mind, so as to induce him to make this will?"

"I did not."

"And to those facts you swear?"

"I do."

Then he passed on to the history of the death of the two sailors who had attested the will, and to the account of Augusta's ultimate rescue, finally closing his examination-in-chief just as the clock struck four, whereon the Court adjourned till the following day.

As may be imagined, though things had gone fairly well so far, nobody concerned of our party passed an over-comfortable night. The strain was too great to admit of it; and really they were all glad to find themselves in the court—which was, if possible, even more crowded on the following morning—filled with the hope that that day might see the matter decided one way or the other.

As soon as the Judge had come in, Augusta resumed her place in the witness-box, and the Attorney-General rose to cross-examine her.

"You told the Court, Miss Smithers, at the conclusion of your evidence, that you are now engaged to be married to Mr. Meeson, the plaintiff. Now, I am sorry to have to put a personal question to you, but I must ask you—Were you at the time of the tattooing of the will, in love with Mr. Meeson?"

This was a home-thrust, and poor Augusta coloured up beneath it; however, her native wit came to her aid.

"If you will define, Sir, what being in love is, I will do my best to answer your question," she said. Whereat the audience, including his Lordship, smiled.

The Attorney-General looked puzzled, as well he might; for there are some things which are beyond the learning of even an Attorney-General.

"Well," he said, "were you matrimonially inclined towards Mr. Meeson?"

"Surely, Mr. Attorney-General," said the Judge, "the one thing does not necessarily include the other?"

"I bow to your Lordship's experience," said Mr. Attorney, tartly. "Perhaps I had better put my question in this way—Had you, at any time, any prospect of becoming engaged to Mr. Meeson?"

"None whatever."

"Did you submit to this tattooing, which must have been painful, with a view of becoming engaged to the plaintiff?"

"Certainly not. I may point out," she added, with hesitation, "that such a disfigurement is not likely to add to anybody's attractions."

"Please answer my questions, Miss Smithers, and do not comment on them. How did you come, then, to submit yourself to such a disagreeable operation?"

"I submitted to it because I thought it right to do so, there being no other apparent means at hand of attaining the late Mr. Meeson's end. Also"—and she paused.

"Also what?"

"Also I had a regard for Mr. Eustace Meeson, and I knew that he had lost his inheritance through a quarrel about myself."

"Ah! now we are coming to it. Then you were tattooed out of regard for the plaintiff, and not purely in the interests of justice?"

"Yes; I suppose so."

"Well, Mr. Attorney," interposed the Judge, "and what if she was?"

"My object, my Lord, was to show that this young lady was not the purely impassive medium in this matter that my learned friend, Mr. Short, would lead the Court to believe. She was acting from motive."

"Most people do," said the Judge drily. "But it does not follow that the motive was an improper one."

Then the learned gentleman continued his cross-examination, directing all the ingenuity of his practised mind to trying to prove by Augusta's admissions, first, that the testator was acting under the undue influence of herself; and secondly, that when the will was executed he was *non compos mentis*. To this end he dwelt at great length on every detail of the events between the tattooing of the will and the death of the testator on the following day, making as much as was possible out of the fact that he died in a fit of mania. But do what he would, he could not shake her evidence upon any material point, and when at last he sat down James Short felt that his case had not received any serious blow.

Then a few more questions having been asked in cross-examination by various other counsel, James rose to re-examine, and, with the object of rebutting the presumption of the testator's mental unsoundness, made Augusta repeat all the details of the confession that the late publisher had made to her as regards his methods of trading. It was beautiful to see the fury and horror portrayed upon the countenance of the choleric Mr. Addison and the cadaverous Mr. Roscoe, when they saw the most cherished secrets of the customs of the trade, as practised at Meeson's, thus paraded in the open light of day, while a dozen swift-pencilled reporters took every detail down.

Then at last Augusta was told to stand down, which she did thankfully enough, and Mrs. Thomas, the wife of Captain Thomas, was called. She proved the finding of Augusta on the island, and that she had seen the hat of one of the sailors, and the rum-cask two-thirds empty, and also produced the shell out of which the men had drunk the rum (which shell the Judge had called Augusta to identify). What was most important, however, was that she gave the most distinct evidence that she had herself seen the late Mr. Meeson interred, and identified the body as that of the late publisher by picking out his photograph from among a bundle of a dozen that were handed to her. Also she swore that when Augusta came aboard the whaler the tattoo marks on her back were not healed.

No cross-examination of the witness worth the name having been attempted, James called a clerk from the office of the late owners of the R.M.S. Kangaroo, who produced the roll of the ship, on which the names of the two sailors, Johnnie Butt and Bill Jones, duly appeared.

This closed the plaintiff's case, and the Attorney-General at once proceeded to call his witnesses, reserving his remarks till the conclusion of the evidence. He had only two witnesses, Mr. Todd, the lawyer who drew and attested the will of Nov. 10, and his clerk, who also attested it, and their examination did not take long. In cross-examination, however, both these witnesses admitted that the testator was in a great state of passion when he executed the will, and gave details of the lively scene that then occurred.

Then the Attorney-General rose to address the Court for the defendants. He said there were two questions before the Court, reserving, for the present, the question as to the admissibility of the evidence of Augusta Smithers; and those were—first, did the tattoo marks upon the lady's neck constitute a will at all? and secondly, supposing that they did, was it proved to the satisfaction of the Court that these undated marks were duly executed by a sane and uninfluenced man, in the presence of the witnesses, as required by the statute. He maintained, in the first place, that these marks were no will within the meaning of the statute; but, feeling that he was not on very sound ground on this point, quickly passed on to the other aspects of the case. With much force and ability he dwelt upon the strangeness of the whole story, and how it rested solely upon the evidence of one witness, Augusta Smithers. It was only if the Court accepted her evidence as it stood that it could come to the conclusion that the will was executed at all, or, indeed, that the two attesting witnesses were on the island at all. Considering the relations which existed between this witness and the plaintiff, was the Court prepared to accept her evidence in this unreserved way? Was it prepared to decide that this will, in favour of a man with whom the testator had violently quarrelled, and had disinherited in consequence of that quarrel, was not, if indeed it was executed at all, extorted by this lady from a weak and dying, and possibly a deranged, man? and with this question the learned gentleman sat down.

He was followed briefly by the Solicitor-General and Mr. Fiddlestick; but though they talked fluently enough, addressing themselves to various minor points, they had nothing fresh of interest to adduce, and finishing at half-past three, James rose to reply on the whole case on behalf of the plaintiff.

There was a moment's pause while he was arranging his notes, and then, just as he was about to begin, the Judge said quietly, "Thank you, Mr. Short, I do not think that I need trouble you," and James sat down with a gasp, for he knew that the cause was won.

Then his Lordship began, and, after giving a masterly summary of the whole case, concluded as follows:—"Such are the details of the most remarkable probate cause that I ever remember to have had brought to my notice, either during my career at the Bar or on the Bench. It will be obvious, as the learned Attorney-General has said, that the whole case really lies between two points. Is the document on the back of Augusta Smithers a sufficient will to carry the property? and, if so, is the unsupported story of that lady as to the execution of the document to be believed? Now, what does the law understand by the term 'Will'? Surely it understands some writing that expresses the wish or will of a person as to the disposition of his property after his decease? This writing must be executed with certain formalities; but if it is so executed by a person not labouring under any mental or other disability it is indefeasible, except by the subsequent execution of a fresh testamentary document, or by its destruction or attempted destruction, *animo revocandi*, or by marriage. Subject to these formalities required by the law, the form of the document—provided that its meaning is clear—is immaterial. Now, do the tattoo marks on the back of this lady constitute such a document, and do they convey the true last will or wish of the testator? That is the first point that I have to decide, and I decide it in the affirmative. It is true that it is not usual for testamentary documents to be tattooed upon the skin of a human being; but, because it is not usual, it does not follow that a tattooed document is not a valid one. The ninth section of the Statute of 1 Vic., cap. 26, specifies that no will shall be valid unless it shall be in writing; but cannot this tattooing be considered as writing within the meaning of the Act? I am clearly of opinion that it can, if only on the ground that the material used was ink—a natural ink, it is true, that of the cuttle-fish, but still ink; for I may remark that the natural product of the cuttle-fish was at one time largely used in this country for that very purpose. Further, in reference to this part of the case, it must be borne in mind that the testator was no eccentric being, who from whim or perversity chose this extraordinary method of signifying his wishes as to the disposal of his property. He was a man placed in about as terrible a position as it is possible to conceive. He was, if we are to believe the story of Miss Smithers, most sincerely anxious to revoke a disposition of his property which he now, standing face to face with the greatest issue of this life, recognised to be unjust, and which was certainly contrary to the promptings of nature as experienced by most men. And yet in this terrible strait in which he found himself, and notwithstanding the earnest desire which grew more intense as his vital forces ebbed, he could find absolutely no means of carrying out his wish. At length, however, this plan of tattooing his will upon the living flesh on a younger and stronger person is presented to him, and he eagerly avails himself of it; and the tattooing is duly carried out in his presence and at his desire, and as duly signed and witnessed. Can it be seriously argued that a document so executed does not fulfil the bare requirements of the law? I think that it cannot, and am of opinion that such a document is as much a valid will as though it had been engrossed upon the skin of a sheep, and duly signed and witnessed in the Temple.

"And now I will come to the second point. Is the evidence of Miss Smithers to be believed? First, let us see where it is corroborated. It is clear, from the testimony of Lady Holmhurst, that when on board the ill-fated Kangaroo, Miss Smithers had no tattoo marks upon her shoulders. It is equally clear from the unshaken testimony of Mrs. Thomas, that when she was rescued by the American whaler, her back was marked with tattooing, then in the healing stage—with tattooing which could not possibly have been inflicted by herself or by the child, who was her sole living companion. It is also proved that there was seen upon the island by Mrs. Thomas the dead body of a man, which she was informed was that of Mr. Meeson, and which she here in court identified by means of a photograph. Also, this same witness produced a shell which she picked up in one of the huts, said to be the shell used by the sailors to drink the rum that led to their destruction; and she swore that she saw a sailor's hat lying on the shore. Now, all this is corroborative evidence, and of a sort not to be despised. Indeed, as to one point, that of the approximate date of the execution of the tattooing, it is to my mind final. Still, there does remain an enormous amount that must be accepted or not, according as to whether or no credence can be placed in the unsupported testimony of Miss Smithers, for we cannot call on a child so young as the present Lord Holmhurst, to bear witness in a Court of Justice. If Miss Smithers, for instance, is not speaking the truth when she declares that the signature of the testator was tattooed upon her under his immediate direction, or that it was tattooed in the presence of the two sailors, Butt and Jones, whose signatures were also tattooed in the presence of the testator and of each other—no will at all was executed, and the plaintiff's case collapses, utterly, since, from the very nature of the facts, evidence as to handwriting would, of course, be useless. Now, I approach the decision of this point after anxious thought and some hesitation. It is not a light thing to set aside a formally executed document such as the will of Nov. 10, upon which the defendants rely, and to entirely alter the devolution of a vast amount of property upon the unsupported testimony of a single witness. It seems to me, however, that there are two tests which the Court can more or less set up as standards, wherewith to measure the truth of the matter. The first of these is the accepted probability of the action of an individual under any given set of circumstances, as drawn from our common knowledge of human nature; and the second, the behaviour and tone of the witness, both in the box and in the course of circumstances that led to her appearance there. I will take the last of those two first, and I may as well state, without further delay, that I am convinced of the truth of the story told by Miss Smithers. It would to my mind be impossible for any man, whose intelligence had been trained by years of experience in this and other courts, and whose daily duty it is to discriminate as to the credibility of testimony, to disbelieve the history so circumstantially detailed in the box by Miss Smithers (Sensation). I watched her demeanour both under examination and cross-examination very closely indeed, and I am convinced that she was telling the absolute truth so far as she knew it.

"And now to come to the second point. It has been suggested, as throwing doubt upon Miss Smithers' story, that the existence of an engagement to marry, between her and the plaintiff, may have prompted her to concoct a monstrous fraud for his benefit; and this is suggested although at the time of the execution of the tattooing no such engagement did, as a matter of fact, exist, or was within measurable distance of the parties. It did not exist, said the Attorney-General; but the disposing mind existed: in other words, that she was then 'in love'—if, notwithstanding Mr. Attorney's difficulty in defining it, I may use the term with the plaintiff. This may or may not have been the case. There are some things which it is quite beyond the power of any Judge or Jury to decide, and one of them certainly is—at what exact period of her acquaintance with a future husband a young lady's regard turns into a warmer feeling? But supposing that the Attorney-General is right, and that although she at that moment clearly had no prospect of marrying him, since she had left England to seek her fortune at the Antipodes, the plaintiff was looked upon by this lady with that kind of regard which is supposed to precede the matrimonial contract, the circumstance, in my mind, tells rather in his favour than against him. For in passing I may remark that this young lady has done a thing which is, in its way, little short of heroic; the more so because it has a ludicrous side. She has submitted to an operation which must not only have been painful, but which is and always will be a blot upon her beauty. I am inclined to agree with the Attorney-General when he says that she did not make the sacrifice without a motive, which may have sprung from a keen sense of justice, and of gratitude to the plaintiff for his interference on her behalf, or from a warmer feeling. In either case there is nothing discreditable about it—rather the reverse, in fact; and, taken by itself, there is certainly nothing here to cause me to disbelieve the evidence of Miss Smithers.

"One question only seems to me to remain. Is there anything to show that the testator was not, at the time of the execution of the will, of a sound and disposing mind? and is there anything in his conduct or history to render the hypothesis of his having executed his will so improbable that the Court should take the improbability into account? As to the first point, I can find nothing. Miss Smithers expressly swore that it was not the case; nor was her statement shaken by a very searching cross-examination. She admitted, indeed, that shortly before death he wandered in his mind, and thought that he was surrounded by the shades of authors waiting to be revenged upon him. But it is no uncommon thing for the mind thus to fail at the last, and it is not extraordinary that this dying man should conjure before his brain the shapes of those with some of whom he appears to have dealt harshly during his life. Nor do I consider it in any way impossible that when he felt his end approaching he should have wished to reverse the sentence of his anger, and restore his nephew, whose only offence had been a somewhat indiscreet use of the language of truth, the inheritance to vast wealth of which he had deprived him. Such a course strikes me as being a most natural and proper one, and perfectly in accordance with the first principles of human nature. The whole tale is undoubtedly of a wild and romantic order, and once again illustrates the saying that 'truth is stranger than fiction.' But I have no choice but to accept the fact that the deceased did, by means of tattooing, carried out by his order, legally execute his true last will in favour of his next-of-kin, Eustace H. Meeson, upon the shoulders of Augusta Smithers, on or about the 22nd day of December, 1885. This being so, I pronounce for the will propounded by the plaintiff, and there will be a grant as prayed."

"With costs, my Lord?" asked James, rising.

"No, I am not inclined to go that length. This litigation has arisen through the testator's own act, and the estate must bear the burden."

"If your Lordship pleases," said James, and sat down.

"Mr. Short," said the Judge, clearing his throat, "I do not often speak in such a sense, but I do feel called upon to compliment you upon the way in which you have, single-handed, conducted this case—in some ways one of the strangest and most important that has ever come before me—having for your opponents so formidable an array of learned gentlemen. The performance would have been creditable to anybody of greater experience and longer years; as it is, I believe it to be unprecedented."

James turned colour, bowed, and sat down, knowing that he was a made man, and that it would be his own fault if his future career at the Bar was not now one of almost unexampled prosperity.

CHAPTER XXII.
ST. GEORGE'S, HANOVER-SQUARE.

The Court broke up in confusion, and Augusta, now that the strain was over, noticed with amusement that the dark array of learned counsel who had been fighting with all their strength to win the case of their clients did not seem to be particularly distressed at the reverse that they had suffered, but chatted away gaily as they tied up their papers with scraps of red tape. She did not, perhaps, quite realize that, having done their best and earned their little fees, they did not feel called on to be heart-broken because the Court declined to take the view they were paid to support. But it was a very different matter with Messrs. Addison and Roscoe, who had just seen two millions of money slip from their avaricious grasp. They were rich men already; but that fact did not gild the pill, for the possession of money does not detract from the desire for the acquisition of more. Mr. Addison was purple with fury, and Mr. Roscoe hid his saturnine face in his hands and groaned. Just then the Attorney-General rose, and seeing James Short coming forward to speak to his clients, stopped him, and shook hands with him warmly.

"Let me congratulate you, my dear fellow," he said. "I never saw a case better done. It was a perfect pleasure to me, and I am very glad that the Judge thought fit to compliment you—a most unusual thing, by-the-way. I can only say that I hope that I may have the pleasure of having you as my junior sometimes in the future. By-the-way, if you have no other engagement I wish that you would call round at my chambers to-morrow about twelve."

Mr. Addison, who was close by, overheard this little speech, and a new light broke upon him. With a bound he plunged between James and the Attorney-General.

"I see what it is now," he said, in a voice shaking with wrath, "I've been sold! I am a victim to collusion. You've had five hundred of my money, confound you!" he shouted, almost shaking his fist in the face of his learned and dignified adviser; "and now you are congratulating this man!" and he pointed his finger at James. "You've been bribed to betray me, Sir. You are a rascal! yes, a rascal!"

At this point the learned Attorney-General, forgetting his learning and the exceeding augustness of his position, actually reverted to those first principles of human nature of which the Judge had spoken, and doubled his fist. Indeed, had not Mr. News, utterly aghast at such a sight, rushed up and dragged his infuriated client back, there is no knowing what scandalous thing might not have happened.

But somehow he was got rid of, and everybody melted away, leaving the ushers to go round and collect the blotting-paper and pens which strewed the empty court.

"And now, good people," said Lady Holmhurst, "I think that the best thing that we can do is all to go home and rest before dinner. I ordered it at seven, and it is half-past five. I hope that you will come, too, Mr. Short, and bring your brother with you; for I am sure that you, both of you, deserve your dinner, if ever anybody did."

And so they all went, and a very jolly dinner they had, as well they might. At last, however, it came to an end, and the legal twins departed, beaming like stars with happiness and champagne. And then Lady Holmhurst departed also, and left Eustace and Augusta alone.

"Life is a queer thing," said Eustace; "here this morning I was a publisher's reader at £180 a year; and now, to-night, if this verdict holds, it seems that I am one of the wealthiest men in England."

"Yes, dear," said Augusta, "and with all the world at your feet, for life is full of opportunities to the rich. You have a great future before you, Eustace; I really am ashamed to marry so rich a man."

"My darling," he said, putting his arm round her; "whatever I have I owe to you. Do you know there is only one thing that I fear about all this money, if it really comes to us; and that is that you will be so taken up with what pleasure-seeking people call social duties, and the distribution of it, that you will give up your writing. So many women are like that. Whatever ability they have seems to vanish utterly away upon their wedding-day. They say afterwards that they have no time, but I often think it is because they do not choose to make time."

"Yes," answered Augusta; "but then that is because they do not really love their work, whatever it may be. Those who really love their art as I love mine, with heart and soul and strength, will not be so easily checked. Of course, distractions and cares come with marriage; but, on the other hand, if one marries happily, there comes quiet of mind and cessation from that ceaseless restlessness that is so fatal to good work. You need not fear, Eustace; if I can, I will show the world that you have not married a dullard; and if I can't—why, my dear, it will be because I am one."

"That comes very nicely from the author of 'Jemima's Vow,'" said Eustace, with sarcasm. "Really, my dear, what between your fame as a writer and as the heroine of the shipwreck and of the great will case, I think that I had better take a back seat at once, for I shall certainly be known as the husband of the beautiful and gifted Mrs. Meeson"—

"Oh! no," answered Augusta; "don't be afraid, nobody would dream of speaking slightingly of the owner of two millions of money."

"Well; never mind chaffing about the money," said Eustace; "we haven't got it yet, for one thing. I have got something to ask you."

"I must be going to bed," said Augusta, firmly.

"No—nonsense!" said Eustace. "You are not going," and he caught her by the arm.

"Unhand me, Sir!" said Augusta, with majesty. "Now what do you want, you silly boy?"

"I want to know if you will marry me next week."

"Next week? Good gracious! No," said Augusta. "Why I have not got my things, and, for the matter of that, I am sure I don't know where the money is coming from to pay for them with."

"Things!" said Eustace, with fine contempt. "You managed to live on Kerguelen Land without things, so I don't see why you can't get married without them—though, for the matter of that, I will get anything you want in six hours. I never did hear such bosh as women talk about 'things.' Listen, dear. For Heaven's sake let's get married and have a little quiet! I can assure you that if you don't, your life won't be worth having after this. You will be hunted like a wild thing, and interviewed, and painted, and worried to death; whereas, if you get married—well, it will be better for us in a quiet way, you know."

"Well, there is something in that," said Augusta. "But supposing that there should be an appeal, and the decision should be reversed, what would happen then?"

"Well, then we should have to work for our living—that's all. I have got my billet, and you could write for the press until your five years' agreement with Meeson and Co. has run out. I would put you in the way of that. I see lots of writing people at my shop."

"Well," said Augusta, "I will speak to Bessie about it."

"Oh, of course, Lady Holmhurst will say no," said Eustace, gloomily. "She will think about the 'things'; and, besides, she won't want to lose you before she is obliged."

"That is all that I can do for you, Sir," said Augusta, with decision. "There—come—that's enough! Good-night." And breaking away from him, she made a pretty little curtsey and vanished.

"Now, I wonder what she means to do," meditated Eustace, as the butler brought him his hat. "I really should not wonder if she came round to it. But then, one never knows how a woman will take a thing. If she will, she will, etc., etc."

And now, it may strike the reader as very strange, but, as a matter of fact, ten days from the date of the above conversation, there was a small-and-early gathering at St. George's, Hanover-square, close by. I say "small," for the marriage had been kept quite secret, in order to prevent curiosity-mongers from marching down upon it in their thousands, as they would certainly have done had it been announced that the heroine of the great will case was going to be married. Therefore the party was very select. Augusta had no relations of her own; and so she had asked Dr. Probate, with whom she had struck up a great friendship, to come and give her away; and, though the old gentleman's previous career had had more connection with the undoing of the nuptial tie than with its contraction, he could not find it in his heart to refuse.

"I shall be neglecting my duties, you know, my dear young lady," he said, shaking his head. "It's very wrong—very wrong, for I ought to be at the Registry; but—well, perhaps I can manage to come—very wrong, though—very wrong, and quite out of my line of business! I expect that I shall begin to address the Court—I mean the clergyman—for the petitioner."

And so it came to pass that on this auspicious day the registering was left to look after itself; and, as a matter of history, it may be stated that no question was asked in Parliament about it.

Then there was Lady Holmhurst, looking very pretty in her widow's dress; and her boy Dick, who was in the highest spirits, and bursting with health and wonder at these strange proceedings on the part of his "Auntie"; and, of course, the legal twins brought up the rear.

And there in the vestry stood Augusta in her bridal dress, as sweet a woman as ever the sun shone on; and looking at her beautiful face, Dr. Probate nearly fell in love with her himself. And yet it was a sad face just then. She was happy—very, as a loving woman who is about to be made a wife should be; but when a great joy draws near to us it comes companioned by the shadows of our old griefs.

The highest sort of happiness has a peculiar faculty of recalling to our minds that which has troubled them in the past, the truth being, that extremes in this, as in other matters, will sometimes touch, which would seem to suggest that sorrow and happiness—however varied in their bloom—yet have a common root. Thus it was with Augusta now. As she stood in the vestry there came to her mind a recollection of her dear little sister, and of how she had prophesied happy greatness and success for her. Now the happiness and the success were at hand, and there in the aisle stood her own true love; but yet the recollection of that dear face, and of the little mound that covered it, rested on them like a shadow. It passed with a sigh, and in its place there came the memory of poor Mr. Tombey, but for whom she would not have been standing there a bride, and of his last words as he put her into the boat. He was food for fishes now, poor fellow, and she was left alone with a great and happy career opening out before her—a career in which her talents would have free space to work. And yet how odd to think it: two or three score of years and it would all be one, and she would be as Mr. Tombey was. Poor Mr. Tombey! perhaps it was as well that he was not there to see her happiness; and let us hope that wherever it is we go after the last event we lose sight of the world and those we knew therein. Otherwise there must be more hearts broken in heaven above than in earth beneath.

"Now, then, Miss Smithers," broke in Dr. Probate, "for the very last time—nobody will call you that again, you know—take my arm; his Lordship—I mean the parson—is there."

It was done, and they were man and wife. Well, even the happiest marriage is always a good thing to get over. It was not a long drive back to Hanover-square, and the very first sight that greeted them on their arrival was the infant from the City (John's), accompanied by his brother, the infant from Pump-court (James'), who had, presumably, come to show him the way, or more probably because he thought that there would be eatables going—holding in his hand a legal-looking letter.

"Marked '*immediate*,' Sir; so I thought that I had better serve it at once," said the first infant, handing the letter to John.

"What is it?" asked Eustace, nervously. He had grown to hate the sight of a lawyer's letter with a deadly hate.

"Notice of appeal, I expect," said John.

"Open it, man!" said Eustace, "and let's get it over."

Accordingly, John did so, and read as follows:—

"MEESON *v.* ADDISON AND ANOTHER

"Dear Sir,—After consultation with our clients, Messrs. Addison and Roscoe, we are enabled to make you the following offer. If no account is required of the mesne profits"—

"That's a wrong term," said James, irritably. "Mesne profits refer to profits derived from real estate. Just like a solicitor to make such a blunder."

"The term is perfectly appropriate," replied his twin, with warmth. "There was some real estate, and, therefore, the term can properly be applied to the whole of the income."

"For Heaven's sake, don't argue but get on!" said Eustace. "Don't you see that I am on tenterhooks?"

"—my clients," continued John, "are ready to undertake that no appeal shall be presented to the recent case of Meeson *v.* Addison and Another. If, however, the plaintiff insists upon an account, the usual steps will be taken to bring the matter before a higher court.—Obediently yours,

"NEWS AND NEWS.
John Short, Esq.

"P.S.—An immediate reply will oblige."

"Well, Meeson, what do you say to that?" said John; "but I beg your pardon, I forgot; perhaps you would like to take counsel's advice," and he pointed to James, who was rubbing his bald head indignantly.

"Oh, no, I should not," answered Eustace; "I've quite made up my mind. Let them stick to their mesne" (here James made a face); "Well, then, to their middle or intermediate or their anything else profits. No appeals for me, if I can avoid it. Send News a telegram."

"That," began James, in his most solemn and legal tones, "is a view of the matter in which I am glad to be able to heartily coincide, although it seems to me that there are several points, which I will touch on one by one."

"Good gracious! no," broke in Lady Holmhurst; "but I think it is rather *mean* of them, don't you, Mr. Short?"

James looked puzzled. "I do not quite take Lady Holmhurst's point," he said plaintively.

"Then you must be stupid," said Eustace, "Don't you see the joke?—'*mesne* profits,' *mean* of them?"

"Ah," said James, with satisfaction; "I perceive. Lady Holmhurst does not seem to be aware that although 'mesne'—a totally erroneous word—is pronounced 'mean,' it is spelt m-e-s-n-e."

"I stand corrected," said Lady Holmhurst, with a little curtsey. "I thought that Mr. James Short would take my ignorance into account, and understand what I *mean*!"

This atrocious pun turned the laugh against the learned James, and then, the telegram to News and News having been dispatched, they all went in to the wedding breakfast.

In a general way, wedding breakfasts are not particularly lively affairs. There is a mock hilarity about them that does not tend to true cheerfulness, and those of the guests who are not occupied with graver thoughts are probably thinking of the dyspepsia that comes after. But this particular breakfast was an exception. For the first time since her husband's unfortunate death, Lady Holmhurst seemed to have entirely recovered her spirits and was her old self, and a very charming self it was, so charming, indeed, that even James forgot his learning and the responsibilities of his noble profession and talked like an ordinary Christian. Indeed, he even went so far as to pay her an elephantine compliment; but as it was three sentences long, and divided into points, it shall not be repeated here.

And then, at length, Dr. Probate rose to propose the bride's health; and very nicely he did it, as might have been expected from a man with his extraordinary familiarity with matrimonial affairs. His speech was quite charming, and aptly sprinkled with classical quotations.

"I have often," he ended, "heard it advanced that all men are in reality equally favoured by the Fates in their passage through the world. I have always doubted the truth of that assertion, and now I am convinced of its falsity. Mr. Eustace is a very excellent young man, and, if I may be allowed to say so, a very good-looking young man; but what, I would ask this assembled company, has Mr. Meeson done above the rest of men to justify his supreme good fortune? Why should this young gentleman be picked out from the multitude of young gentlemen to inherit two millions of money, and to marry the most charming—yes, the most charming, the most talented, and the bravest young lady that I have ever met—a young lady who not only carries twenty fortunes on her face, but another fortune in her brain, and his fortune on her neck—and such a fortune, too! Sir"—and he bowed towards Eustace—

"'Lovely Thais sits beside thee,
Take the goods the gods provide thee.'

"I salute you, as all men must salute one so supremely favoured. Humbly, I salute you; humbly I pray that you may continually deserve the almost unparalleled good that it has pleased Providence to bestow upon you."

And then Eustace rose and made his speech, and a very good speech it was, considering the trying circumstances under which it was made. He told them how he had fallen in love with Augusta's sweet face the very first time that he had set eyes upon it in the office of his uncle at Birmingham. He told them what he had felt when, after getting some work in London, he had returned to Birmingham to find his lady-love flown, and of what he had endured when he heard that she was among the drowned on board the Kangaroo. Then he came to the happy day of the return, and to that still happier day when he discovered that he had not loved her in vain, finally ending thus—

"Dr. Probate has said that I am a supremely fortunate man, and I admit the truth of his remark. I am, indeed, fortunate above my deserts, so fortunate that I feel afraid. When I turn and see my beloved wife sitting at my side, I feel afraid lest I should after all be dreaming a dream, and awake to find nothing but emptiness. And then, on the other hand, is this colossal wealth, which has come to me through her, and there again I feel afraid. But, please Heaven, I hope with her help to do some good with it, and remembering always that it is a great trust that has been placed in my hands. And she also is a trust and a far more inestimable one, and as I deal with her so may I be dealt with here and hereafter." Then, by an afterthought, he proposed the health of the legal twins, who had so nobly borne the brunt of the affray single-handed, and disconcerted the Attorney-General and all his learned host.

Thereon James rose to reply in terms of elephantine eloquence, and would have gone through the whole case again had not Lady Holmhurst in despair pulled him by the sleeve and told him that he must propose her health, which he did with sincerity, lightly alluding to the fact that she was a widow by describing her as being in a "discovert condition, with all the rights and responsibilities of a 'femme sole.'"

Everybody burst out laughing, not excepting poor lady Holmhurst herself, and James sat down, not without indignation that a giddy world should object to an exact and legal definition of the status of the individual as set out by the law.

And after that Augusta went and changed her dress, and then came the hurried good-byes; and, to escape observation, they drove off in a hansom cab amidst a shower of old shoes.

And there in that hansom cab we will leave them.

CHAPTER XXIII.
MEESON'S ONCE AGAIN.

A month had passed—a month of long, summer days and such happiness as young people who truly love each other can get out of a honeymoon spent under the most favourable circumstances in the sweetest, sunniest spots of the Channel Islands. And now the curtain draws up for the last time in this history, where it drew up for the first—in the inner office of Meeson's huge establishment.

During the last fortnight certain communications had passed between Mr. John Short, being duly authorized thereto, and the legal representatives of Messrs. Addison and Roscoe, with the result that the interests of these gentlemen in the great publishing house had been bought up, and that Eustace Meeson was now the sole owner of the vast concern, which he intended to take under his personal supervision.

Now, accompanied by John Short, whom he had appointed to the post of his solicitor both of his business and his private affairs, and by Augusta, he was engaged in formally taking over the keys from the head manager, who was known throughout the establishment, as No. 1.

"I wish to refer to the authors' agreements of the early part of last year," said Eustace.

No. 1 produced them somewhat sulkily. He did not like the appearance of this determined young owner upon the scene, with his free and un-Meeson-like ways.

Eustace turned them over, and while he did so, his happy wife stood by him, marvelling at the kaleidoscopic changes in her circumstances. When last she had stood in that office, not a year ago, it had been as a pitiful suppliant begging for a few pounds wherewith to try and save her sister's life, and now—

Suddenly Eustace stopped turning, and drawing a document from the bundle, glanced at it. It was Augusta's agreement with Meeson and Co. for "Jemima's Vow," the agreement binding her to them for five years which had been the cause of all her troubles, and, as she firmly believed, of her little sister's death.

"There, my dear," said Eustace to his wife, "there is a present for you. Take it!"

Augusta took the document, and having looked to see what it was, shivered as she did so. It brought the whole thing back so painfully to her mind.

"What shall I do with it," she asked; "tear it up?"

"Yes," he answered. "No, stop a bit," and taking it from her he wrote "cancelled" in big letters across it, signed and dated it.

"There," he said, "now send it to be framed and glazed, and it shall be hung here in the office, to show how they used to do business at Meeson's."

No. 1 snorted, and looked at Eustace aghast. What would the young man be after next?

"Are the gentlemen assembled in the hall?" asked Eustace of him when the remaining documents were put away again.

No. 1 said that they were, and accordingly, to the hall they went, wherein were gathered all the editors, sub-editors, managers, sub-managers of the various departments, clerks, and other employees, not forgetting the tame authors, who, a pale and mealy regiment, had been marched up thither from the Hutches, and the tame artists with flying hair—and were now being marshalled in lines by No. 1, who had gone on before. When Eustace and his wife and John Short got to the top of the hall, where some chairs had been set, the whole multitude bowed, whereon he begged them to be seated—a permission of which the tame authors, who sat all day in their little wooden hutches, and sometimes a good part of the night also, did not seem to care to avail themselves of. But the tame artists, who had, for the most part, to work standing, sat down readily.

"Gentlemen," said Eustace, "first let me introduce you to my wife, Mrs. Meeson, who, in another capacity, has already been—not greatly to her own profit—connected with this establishment, having written the best work of fiction that has ever gone through our printing-presses"—(Here some of the wilder spirits cheered, and Augusta blushed and bowed)—"and who will, I hope and trust, write many even better books, which we shall have the honour of giving to the world." (Applause.) "Also, gentlemen, let me introduce you to Mr. John Short, my solicitor, who, together with his twin brother, Mr. James Short, brought the great lawsuit in which I was engaged to a successful issue.

"And now I have to tell you why I have summoned you all to meet me here. First of all, to say that I am now the sole owner of this business, having bought out Messrs. Addison and Roscoe"—("And a good job too," said a voice)—"and that I hope we shall work well together; and secondly, to inform you that I am going to totally revolutionise the course of business as hitherto practised in this establishment"—(Sensation)—"having, with the assistance of Mr. Short, drawn up a scheme for that purpose. I am informed in the statement of profits on which the purchase price of the shares of Messrs. Addison and Roscoe was calculated, that the average net profits of this house during the last ten years have amounted to fifty-seven and a fraction per cent on the capital invested. Now, I have determined that in future the net profits of any given undertaking shall be divided as follows:—Ten per cent to the author of the book in hand, and ten per cent to the House. Then, should there be any further profit, it will be apportioned thus: One-third—of which a moiety will go towards a pension fund—to the employés of the House, the division to be arranged on a fixed scale"—(Enormous sensation, especially among the tame authors)—"and the remainder to the author of the work. Thus, supposing that a book paid cent. per cent., I shall take ten per cent., and the employés would take twenty-six and a fraction per cent., and the author would take sixty-four per cent."

And here an interruption occurred. It came from No. 1, who could no longer retain his disgust.

"I'll resign," he said; "I'll resign! Meeson's content with ten per cent, and out-of-pocket expenses, when an author—a mere author—gets sixty! It's shameful—shameful!"

"If you choose to resign, you can," said Eustace, sharply; "but I advise you to take time to think it over. Gentlemen," went on Eustace, "I daresay that this seems a great change to you, but I may as well say at once that I am no wild philanthropist. I expect to make it pay, and pay well. To begin with, I shall never undertake any work that I do not think will pay—that is, without an adequate guarantee, or in the capacity of a simple agent; and my own ten per cent will be the first charge on the profits; then the author's ten. Of course, if I speculate in a book, and buy it out and out, subject to the risks, the case will be different. But with a net ten per cent certain, I am, like people in any other line of business, quite prepared to be satisfied; and, upon those terms, I expect to become the publisher of all the best writers in England, and I also expect that any good writer will in future be able to make a handsome income out of his work. Further, it strikes me that you will most of you find yourselves better off at the end of the year than you do at present" (Cheers). "One or two more matters I must touch on. First and foremost the Hutches, which I consider a scandal to a great institution like this, will be abolished"—(Shouts of joy from the tame authors)—"and a handsome row of brick chambers erected in their place, and, further, their occupants will in future receive a very permanent addition to their salaries "—(renewed and delirious cheering). "Lastly, I will do away with this system—this horrid system—of calling men by numbers, as though they were convicts instead of free Englishmen. Henceforth everybody in this establishment will be known by his own name." (Loud cheers.)

"And now one more thing: I hope to see you all at dinner at Pompadour Hall this day next week, when we will christen our new scheme and the new firm, which, however, in the future as in the past, will be known as Meeson & Co., for, as we are all to share in the profits of our undertaking, I consider that we shall still be a company, and I hope a prosperous and an honest company in the truest sense of the word." And then amidst a burst of prolonged and rapturous cheering, Eustace and his wife bowed, and were escorted out to the carriage that was waiting to drive them to Pompadour Hall.

In half-an-hour's time they were re-entering the palatial gates from which, less than a year before, Eustace had been driven forth to seek his fortune. There, on either side, were drawn up the long lines of menials, gorgeous with plush and powder (for Mr. Meeson's servants had never been discharged), and there was the fat butler, Johnson, at their head, the same who had given his farewell message to his uncle.

"Good gracious!" said Augusta, glancing up the marble steps, "there are six of those great footmen. What on earth shall I do with them all"—

"Sack them," said Eustace, abruptly; "the sight of those overfed brutes makes me sick!"

And then they were bowed in—and under the close scrutiny of many pairs of eyes, wandered off with what dignity they could command to dress for dinner.

In due course they found themselves at dinner, and such a dinner! It took an hour and twenty minutes to get through, or rather the six footmen took an hour and twenty minutes to carry the silver dishes in and out. Never since their marriage had Eustace and Augusta felt so miserable.

"I don't think that I like being so rich," said Augusta rising and coming down the long table to her husband, when at last Johnson had softly closed the door. "It oppresses me!"

"So it does me," said Eustace; "and I tell you what it is, Gussie," he went on, putting his arm round her, "I won't stand having all these infernal fellows hanging round me. I shall sell this place, and go in for something quieter."

And at that moment there came a dreadful diversion. Suddenly, and without the slightest warning, the doors at either end of the room opened. Through the one came two enormous footmen laden with coffee and cream, etc., and through the other Johnson and another powdered monster bearing cognac and other liquors. And there was Augusta with Eustace's arm round her, absolutely too paralysed to stir. Just as the men came up she got away somehow, and stood looking like an idiot, while Eustace coloured to his eyes. Indeed, the only people who showed no confusion were those magnificent menials, who never turned a single powdered hair, but went through their solemn rites with perfectly unabashed countenances.

"I can't stand this," said Augusta, feebly, when they had at length departed. "I am going to bed; I feel quite faint."

"All right," said Eustace, "I think that it is the best thing to do in this comfortless shop. Confound that fellow, Short, why couldn't he come and dine? I wonder if there is any place where one could go to smoke a pipe, or rather a cigar—I suppose those fellows would despise me if I smoked a pipe? There was no smoking allowed here in my uncle's time, so I used to smoke in the house-keeper's room; but I can't do that now"—

"Why don't you smoke here?—the room is so big it would not smell," said Augusta.

"Oh, hang it all, no," said Eustace; "think of the velvet curtains! I can't sit and smoke by myself in a room fifty feet by thirty; I should get the blues. No, I shall come upstairs, too, and smoke there"—

And he did.

Early, very early in the morning, Augusta woke, got up, and put on a dressing-gown.

The light was streaming through the rich gold cloth curtains, some of which she had drawn. It lit upon the ewers, made of solid silver, on the fine lace hangings of the bed, and the priceless inlaid furniture, and played round the faces of the cupids on the frescoed ceiling. Augusta stared at it all and then thought of the late master of this untold magnificence as he lay dying in the miserable hut in Kerguelen Land. What a contrast was here!

"Eustace," she said to her sleeping spouse, "wake up, I want to say something to you."

"Eh! what's the matter?" said Eustace, yawning.

"Eustace, we are too rich—we ought to do something with all this money."

"All right," said Eustace, "I'm agreeable. What do you want to do?"

"I want to give away a good sum—say, two hundred thousand, that isn't much out of all you have—to found an institution for broken-down authors."

"All right," said Eustace; "only you must see about it, I can't be bothered. By-the-way," he added, waking up a little, "you remember what the old boy told you when he was dying? I think that starving authors who have published with Meeson's ought to have the first right of election."

"I think so, too," said Augusta, and she went to the buhl writing-table to work out that scheme on paper which, as the public is aware, is now about to prove such a boon to the world of scribblers.

"I say, Gussie!" suddenly said her husband. "I've just had a dream!"

"Well!" she said sharply, for she was busy with her scheme; "what is it?"

"I dreamt that James Short was a Q.C., and making twenty thousand a year, and that he had married Lady Holmhurst."

"I should not wonder if that came true," answered Augusta, biting the top of her pen.

Then came another pause.

"Gussie," said Eustace, sleepily, "are you quite happy?"

"Yes, of course I am, that is, I should be if it wasn't for those footmen and the silver water-jugs."

"I wonder at that," said her husband.

"Why?"

"Because"—(yawn)—"of that will upon your neck"—(yawn). "I should not have believed that a woman could be quite happy"—(yawn)—"who could—never go to Court."

And he went to sleep again; while, disdaining reply, Augusta worked on.

THE END.

www.ingramcontent.com/pod-product-compliance
Lightning Source LLC
LaVergne TN
LVHW090404051026
849518LV00006B/2230